FANGS LIKE ME

Lyssa Dering

Lane, a newborn vampire, still feels the pain of betrayal. Two years ago, a faithless boyfriend took his life, and now, Lane's Maker has also left him behind. The pain of separation burns strong when all Lane wants are arms to hold him and enough warm blood to satisfy his voracious appetite. At a shifter party, Lane is drawn to a hunky Alpha werewolf who tries to console him.

Parker is more than a thoughtless hookup. Since his family disowned him for finding boys just as hot as girls, all he wants is someone to love and look after. The sweet little vamp calls to his protective instincts, but he sure is jumpy. Cuddling with boys is new and delicious, but when this boy also wants him as a food source, things get complicated.

Vampires and shifters aren't supposed to get along, and Parker's rough dominance triggers bad memories for Lane. But Parker's wolf wants Lane, and he knows he can give Lane what he needs. Can Lane learn to navigate his past and give the thing growing between them a chance? Or will the very real possibilities of heartache, abandonment, and even death, keep them apart?

Published by
NineStar Press
PO Box 91792
Albuquerque, New Mexico, 87199
www.ninestarpress.com

Warning: This book contains sexually explicit content which is only suitable for mature readers.

Print ISBN #978-1-945952-73-9
Cover by Natasha Snow
Edited by Elizabetta

CHAPTER ONE

Lane owed his Maker everything, so he had no right to be sad. Except the Maker/progeny Bond that had been a pain in his ass (not literally, unfortunately) since Theo had saved his life ensured that he would be sad, regardless. Theo had gone off to some vampire summit just last night, and he would be gone for a whole year. Lane, "babyvamp" that he was, was not important enough to go to a summit. As everybody in the den kept telling him, he had to learn to survive distance with his Maker eventually. It still hurt like a cracked sternum, though.

Maybe Lane had accepted the invitation to this shifter party as a fuck-you to Theo and his other denmates. Or maybe it had been Heather's good-natured prodding that had brought him to the alley behind her house in Ferndale. She'd said he shouldn't be alone right now, which was true. But he wasn't sure if being in a house full of shifters was going to be all that helpful. He'd been to her house a few times before when other shifters were present. A good few of them hated vampires and had no qualms about giving him dirty looks whenever he showed. *"They're more open-minded than you think,"* she'd told him over and over, but those looks said different.

Prime example: the shifter smoking on the back porch.

Brown and orange leaves crunched under Lane's sneakers as he ascended the wooden stairs, and he shoved his hands into the pockets of his hoodie. He didn't need the hoodie; he was impervious to the temperamental Michigan weather, after all, but it was best to keep up appearances.

The shifter was tall and fit, dressed in a flannel shirt and gray beanie. Lane had to edge past him to get to the sliding double doors that led into the living room. As he did so, the shifter's confident gaze landed on him. Behind smoke tendrils, his eyes glowed orange.

Lane's skin broke out in goose pimples—his vampire instincts telling him there was a threat here.

"Problem?" The shifter exposed his eyeteeth with a crooked grin.

Lane shook his head and hurried inside.

As soon as the soles of his sneakers hit the carpet, pleasant warmth washed over his cold skin, getting rid of those goose pimples. Shifters burned even hotter than humans, and there were a lot of them packed inside the house. A few of them were around the coffee table, playing what appeared to be Euchre, but most of them merely sat around talking.

Lane headed past them, looking for Heather and her head of dirty-blonde waves. He found her in the kitchen. She was spraying whipped cream into glasses filled with coffee-colored liquid.

"Who's the guy smoking outside?" Lane knew Heather hated being around smokers; like many shifters, she disliked the smell. Lane didn't mind it, even though he also had enhanced senses. His denmate Erica smoked out of a vintage cigarette holder like Cruella de Vil.

"Parker. He's new. Want a shot?" Heather dipped a finger into one of the glasses and sucked whipped cream off her glossy nail.

Lane scrunched his nose. "No, thanks." He preferred hard liquor. He opened one of the cabinets, found some vodka, and took several swallows straight from the bottle before wiping his mouth on his sleeve.

"Trying to get drunk?" asked Heather.

"Yeah. Fuck everything." He'd have to wake up his heart to get drunk, but pouring the liquor down his throat was the first order of business. He needed to drown the ache in his chest. He needed to forget the hard line of Theo's shoulders and the way his curls looked after he got out of the shower, dark and shining. How he'd lock eyes with Lane sometimes and—

"You should try talking to some people," said Heather. "You need to make some friends."

"You're my friend, aren't you?"

She gave Lane a knowing, playful look that probably would have melted some guys.

Lane screwed the cap back on the vodka bottle and headed toward the hallway, where the bathroom was. There were only two ways to get his heart to start beating, and he needed to be alone for one of them. Or with someone else, but that wasn't happening. Not unless it was Theo, who was 1) not interested, and 2) on the other side of the world.

He was about a foot from the bathroom door when he stopped and gasped. The goose pimples sprouted back up, and his heart kicked into life. *Wolf. Threat.*

But this was a shifter party. Just because it usually happened much later at night didn't mean they couldn't shift now. Lane closed his eyes and took a slow breath. He registered the scent of cigarette smoke as the alcohol swam in his bloodstream, egged on by the heavy, unnatural thud of his vampire heart.

"Parker?" he said softly. The wolf's orange eyes matched those of the smoker outside. "You scared me."

The wolf stalked forward and sat at Lane's feet, nudging Lane's palm with his hot, wet nose. Lane's denmates had said wolves were the most dangerous of shifters, because they had large, sharp teeth and the strength to rip off a vampire's head. Theo and Erica wouldn't allow Heather inside the den, but they didn't mind Lane hanging out with her. She was a house cat when she shifted, and her teeth were small.

Wolves didn't usually come to these parties. They stuck close to their own kind like vampires were supposed to. But Heather had said Parker was new...

Parker tongued between Lane's fingers. Lane should have taken his hand away, probably, but it felt good, like a warm bath.

His heart slowed but didn't go quiet. *Thump... Thump... Thump...* He closed his eyes. Parker licked the sensitive underside of his wrist, and Lane wished he didn't have to stand anymore.

After a few seconds, the wet heat disappeared. Lane opened his eyes to find Parker still in wolf form, but a few feet away now and looking back at him expectantly. Was Lane supposed to follow? When he took a few steps forward, Parker headed into a bedroom, so Lane followed him there, too.

Parker hopped up onto the bed.

Oh God. Does he want to...? From what Lane had seen so far, Parker looked like the quintessential frat boy, one he would have gladly gotten on his knees for back in college. But a lot had happened since then. His murder, for one.

"I... can't."

Parker rested his chin on his paws and whimpered.

"Oh, come on," said Lane. "What are you gonna do? Lick me some more?"

Parker opened his mouth and stuck his tongue out, panting jovially.

Lane found himself smiling. He couldn't remember the last time he'd done so genuinely, and the movement felt foreign to the muscles in his cheeks. Still, it was the alcohol that gave him the courage to get on the bed. He lay on his back and closed his eyes again.

Fur brushed against his skin. The hot tongue found his ear and lapped until Lane's breath turned shaky. "This is weird," he whispered.

But Parker didn't stop, licking from behind Lane's ear and down the line of his jaw. Lane's fangs cut through his gums at the same time that his dick filled, and he thought, *I'm so screwed up.* Only a screwed-up person would let a shifter do this to them in full shifted form. But it felt good. Lane never got to feel good. He was always having to hold himself back—his hunger, his feelings for Theo, his panic when the memories cropped up.

The fur disappeared, and a decidedly human hand held the opposite side of his face. Lane became uncomfortably aware of the thumping of Parker's heart, yet he turned into him and nuzzled a little, his fangs throbbing along with his cock.

"Still weird?" Parker breathed against his ear.

No, but there was his hunger, and under that, panic. He gripped the comforter where his hands rested at his sides. What if Parker's teeth came out? In all Lane's fantasies about Theo, his Maker's fangs stayed in. Theo was old enough to control them. But Parker was young, like Lane, and he made rash decisions. Like hooking up with complete strangers, apparently.

"Hey." Parker pulled back, his eyes glowing bright and menacing, even as they drooped in concern. "What's wrong?" Lane zeroed in on his mouth as he spoke, as his lips moved over unmistakably lengthened teeth.

"I can't do this." He tried to sit up but wasn't able to do so until Parker got the clue and got off him. Parker was heavier, stronger. Before Lane could flee, Parker grabbed him by the arm, his claws scratching him above the elbow. Parker must have scented Lane's blood as it welled to the surface because he let go and pulled back.

"Look, I'm s—"

Lane sped into the hallway. He moved toward the living room with escape on his mind, slowing to a frustrating human pace so he wouldn't alarm the shifters. Already they would see his exposed fangs, dilated eyes, and dark red tears. He didn't need to call extra attention to himself.

Outside in the alley, he allowed himself one deep breath of the now cooler late-autumn air. Then he sped into the darkness toward home. He'd text Heather later to let her know he'd left, but he wasn't sure he'd be able to go back to her house again. Not if Parker was there, anyway, with anecdotal evidence of just how fucked-up Lane was.

* * *

Parker plopped down into one of the easy chairs in the living room and crossed his arms. He had a bone to pick with Heather, but she was on the couch, making out with that little mouse shifter, Rina. Parker couldn't help but watch out of the corner of his eye. Rina wasn't much to look at, but Heather was all soft curves, milky skin, and a lacy pink bra peeking out of her V-neck. In between kisses, they giggled and breathed, and then Heather pulled away to check her phone.

Seizing the opportunity, Parker said, "I can't *believe* you didn't tell me a vampire was coming."

Heather looked up from her phone and pierced him with one of her cold stares. Her eyes were the same eerie green whether she was in her human or feline form. "Is this your fault?" she said, holding the screen toward him.

"Huh?" Parker leaned forward to try to see what she was talking about, but she whisked the phone away and began typing furiously.

"Lane left. Did you say something to him?"

Parker laughed. *Lane, is it?* "Not really. Wait—" He perked up. "Is he talking about me?"

"No."

Even though Heather was all scary tension, Rina leaned her head on Heather's shoulder and closed her eyes. Probably she was drunk. Parker had only met her a few weeks ago, but he'd never seen her that affectionate with anybody. She barely talked, and when she did, it was only to Heather. Typical mouse.

Parker wanted that, though—somebody not afraid to be near him even when he was emotional. Clearly the little vamp wasn't a prospect if he couldn't handle some claws during sex. Or else, it *would* have been sex if he'd let things get that far.

"What's he saying then?" Parker asked anyway.

"He's upset," said Heather. "Thinks he shouldn't come to any more of our parties."

"Oh." *Because of me?* Parker creased his brows. He and guilt had become best friends over the last year, but it was the last thing he'd expected to feel tonight. Sure, he'd been regretful when Lane had pulled away, earlier in the bedroom. But Parker hadn't done anything. Aside from that little scratch, which had clearly been an accident. "Give me his number."

"Why?"

"We might've..." Parker winced and swiped a hand over his buzzed hair. "We almost hooked up."

"Parker! I leave you alone for like twenty minutes—"

"I'll set him straight, okay? And you won't have to worry about it." Parker got out his phone.

"Fine." Heather's pupils turned to slits. She chucked her phone at Parker's chest. "Be nice to him, though. He's dealing with some heavy vampire shit."

Heather knew full well *Parker* was dealing with some heavy shit. Heavy werewolf shit. She'd been the one to take him in when he left his pack a few weeks ago. This was the second party she'd hosted since then; the vampire—Lane—hadn't been at the last one. Every single other guest was a shifter of some kind. They were solitary animals like Heather's house cat, or pariahs like Parker's wolf—too queer for the family, unfit to mate.

Once he'd taken down Lane's number, Parker set Heather's phone on the arm of the couch. He gritted his teeth and went outside onto the porch, trying to think what to send to Lane.

Really, he wasn't good at texting or fixing things with anyone. The last texts he'd sent aside from the one to Heather yesterday (*Do you want me to pick up some Lactaid on the way home?*) had been to his ex-mate Carly, and she hadn't answered any of them. Not that he blamed her; they'd been kind of pathetic. But what if Lane didn't answer?

Parker growled softly at himself. He was being weak. He was an Alpha. Alphas took care of business.

He tapped a quick message, hit SEND, and took out his lighter and a cigarette.

* * *

Theo's den was a social hub for his clique of vampires much like Heather's house was a gathering spot for her shifter friends. But while Heather let the occasional nonshifter into her parties, Theo only welcomed vampires and the humans who knew about them. In order to access the driveway that led to the den's mansion, one had to be put on a list, or as with Lane, have a key card. He swiped his at the gated entrance, smiling at its human attendant, and sped up the hill to where the mansion sat nestled in a cluster of pine trees. While Heather's house was a typically suburban two-bedroom, the den was in the far more upscale Bloomfield Hills and boasted seven bedrooms, eight bathrooms, and a shimmering lakeside view. Neither house was very far from Detroit, but Lane hadn't so much as driven through the city since college, when he'd gone to see Radiohead with the vampire who'd killed him. Adrian.

He'd gotten pretty good at blocking out all thoughts of *him*. But seeing the shifter's fangs so close? In a sexual situation? He shouldn't have drunk that vodka, shouldn't have interacted with Parker at all.

As he passed the fountain out front and ascended the sweeping stairway, he licked his hand and did his best to wipe away what was left of his blood tears. He knew what his denmates would think of him coming home from a shifter party crying. For one, they'd think him naive for being open-minded about warm-blooded species. For two, they'd discount his emotions with a wave of their all-knowing hands. *Newborns. They're so dramatic.* Lane didn't need it. But he was pretty sure any idiot would be able to tell he was freaking. His fangs were still out, his pupils were likely blown wide, and he wanted a drink. But that would require asking Erica to supervise him feeding from a human, or going into the kitchen for a blood bag.

Neither appealed. As soon as he got inside, he made his way up the staircase, managing to get to his room without being caught. In the room next door, he could hear his other denmate, Sam, screwing a human. He could tell it was a human because of how the heartbeat sounded. It seemed to caress his very brain, but Lane fought the hunger. He was getting better and better at that.

He texted Heather before taking off his clothes and getting in bed. All the while, the human heartbeat next door got slower and slower. He tried not to think about teeth, tried to blank out the bad parts of his brain. But it was hard with his fangs aching. He swallowed and pictured Parker instead: the soothing warmth of his wolf's tongue and a breathy whisper against his ear. He inhaled and imagined cigarette smoke burning his nostrils. Tears welled and dripped thickly past his lashes. Trauma was supposed to be easier as a vampire. Some evolutionary thing because of how long they lived. If vampires felt things too deeply, they'd go insane. But Lane still felt insane. He lost the image of Parker and sank into memories of the night he'd gone to that concert: Adrian getting testy in the standing-room-only section, wrapping his cold arms around Lane to keep everyone away. Adrian biting him, making him come during Lane's favorite song.

Lane's phone buzzed. He expected another text from Heather, but it was a number he didn't recognize.

Hey. This is Parker. Got your number from Heather. Are you okay?

Lane's stomach did a flip. His fingers shook as he read and reread the text.

Was he okay? No. But in his experience, people didn't want to hear that.

I'm fine. You don't need to worry about me

Parker's response came lightning fast. *What did I do to make you leave? I didn't mean to claw you.*

Lane looked down at where Parker had scratched him. The wounds had been slight, and they were already healed.

It wasn't that

Then what? Tell me.

Lane blinked at his phone for several seconds. Parker actually cared, didn't he? Or maybe he just liked to get his way. Maybe he was one of those mystical Alphas Heather had mentioned earlier in their friendship, when Lane had "come out" as a vampire to her. He'd met her in college but had had no idea she was supernatural. Immediately they'd traded everything they knew about the other's species. *"House cats don't need Alphas. That's dog and wolf shit,"* she'd said. What Lane had taken away from that bit of information was that if vampires had Alphas, they'd be den leaders. So Theo was his Alpha. He wasn't sure *who* the omegas were.

Lane sighed and decided to tell Parker just enough. No way would he ever tell him the whole pathetic story.

Your teeth scared me. It's stupid. Sorry

You don't have to be sorry. They come out when I'm turned on, but I wasn't going to hurt you.

Next door, Sam's heart had stopped beating, and the human's heart was slow and steady, as if she (or he) were asleep.

Parker sent a second text. *Yours were out.*

Yeah. Same reason

It wasn't a lie, technically. He'd been both scared and turned on. Maybe he didn't want to make Parker feel worse than he already did for something that was Lane's fault. He'd gone into the bedroom. He shouldn't have. That was on him.

Parker sent a smiley face. And then: *Please don't feel like you can't come to Heather's because of me. I'm staying with her right now, but I'll steer clear of you if that's what you want.*

Lane's fangs gave a panicked throb. He didn't want that! Why he didn't want it, though, he wasn't entirely sure.

You don't have to do that. Really. I'm fine

Good. I'm happy to hear that.

Lane took a deep breath and added Parker to his contacts. Then he got up to wash the tears off his face. He hadn't wanted to go feed, but if he didn't—and soon—he was going to lose his shit. Still, nobody downstairs needed to know he'd been crying.

CHAPTER TWO

"Yeah, he's an Alpha. He's not an asshole, though. He's sweet."

Lane sat on the freshly wiped counter at Brewhaha, the cafe where Heather worked as a barista. The cafe was closed now, but she'd been the only one working since it was a slow Sunday night. It was a regular thing for Lane to come and keep her company at the end of the night while she swept and mopped. Since the vampire den took care of all of his basic needs, he didn't need to work himself. Theo had encouraged him from the start to take some time before he decided which dream to pursue first, since he was young and had all the time in the world now. Too bad he didn't have any dreams to choose from. When he'd died, he'd still been a General Studies major because he hadn't really been drawn to anything.

"I didn't say he was an asshole," Lane said.

"So you like him?"

Lane shrugged. "I don't really know him."

Heather zigzagged the mop head over the linoleum behind the counter before rolling the bucket out into the dining area. "I don't really know Rina, and I like her."

Lane smirked. He'd noticed Heather and the mouse had gotten closer lately. He didn't really like it when they made out, but that was more to do with him than them. Public displays of affection made him tense.

He twisted around and dangled his feet on the opposite side of the counter. "So when's the next party?" He tried not to sound too excited about it. He was well aware he'd done a complete one-eighty since talking to Parker last night.

"Trust me. You don't want to go to the next party."

"Oh." Now he tried not to sound too sad. "Why not?"

"It's the day before the full moon. Things get...crazy."

From what Lane had seen of Heather's get-togethers so far, they were pretty chill. But then, he never stayed very long. He'd only been allowed to leave the den without an escort for the last few months, and Theo had made it pretty clear he shouldn't be out at all hours.

"Could you be more specific?" he asked, and winced a little. His mind took him to fangs and claws, fur and animal noises. The way wolves were supposed to swell inside of you so you couldn't get free.

Heather mopped under two whole tables before stopping and leaning on the mop handle. "Okay. I try really hard not to be a prejudiced jerk, so if I'm doing that here, tell me. But vampires are generally, like, straightlaced. Do you know what I mean?"

Lane pictured Sam at the den three nights ago, taking a male human in front of everyone. "No," he said forcefully.

"You're offended."

"A little, yeah."

"I just mean..." Heather sighed and went back to work, making the tiles behind her gleam. "If you ran out on Parker last time, you'd freak if you saw him during the full moon. It's not like mating season, but people will be on edge, and a lot of them will hook up. Parker will probably hook up. It shouldn't be with you."

Heather probably didn't mean it the way it sounded. But Lane's vision clouded with blood at the harsh words.

When Heather looked at him, she stopped mopping again. "Lane..."

"No." He sniffed. "You're right. It's a recipe for disaster all around."

"That's not what I meant. I just think you should take things slow. You've got a lot going on with Theo being—"

Lane hopped off the counter and landed with his hands in fists at his sides. "Don't talk about Theo."

"Okay. Jesus." Heather finished mopping and rolled the bucket around Lane. "I don't want you to get hurt. That's all."

"You said Parker was sweet."

"He is. But he's also a wolf." Heather gave Lane a look that seemed far too much like pity. "If you really want to date a shifter, I have a single friend you might like. Dolphin. No teeth, no claws."

Lane shook his head and sighed through his nose. "I don't care if someone's a shifter, a vamp, a human. Whatever." Except every single option brought issues with it. Would they be able to control their hunger? Would he be able to control his hunger? Would one of them die?

"Parker does," said Heather.

"Huh?" Lane furrowed his brow and followed her into the back room. She splashed the dirty mop water into a white utility sink.

"Parker cares about species. He's got a thing for vamps. I haven't known him that long, to be honest. I didn't know if he was going to be an ass about vampires or not. Turns out…" Heather pursed her lips as she dropped the empty bucket onto the floor. "He loves them."

Lane's heart constricted in his chest, sending blood pumping toward his groin. He'd met humans with vampire fetishes, but they were all submissive. Lane wasn't into submissive. An Alpha with a hard-on for vampires, though? "Gross," he said, even as his cheeks flushed.

* * *

Parker hated the full moon. He used to like it okay, once things got to the running-through-the-woods part. He'd gotten to run side-by-side with his ex-mate Carly, and his Alpha hadn't been thoroughly disappointed in him.

Parker's dad was almost always disappointed about something, but Parker not being "man enough" to take on the breeding mantle and start up a pack of his own was the gravest offense. After he'd broken up with Carly, his dad had given him a thorough talking-to about "ruining both their chances for a strong local partnership." No matter that he was only twenty-five. No matter that there were single wolves all over the place even if they weren't in this area. If Parker really wanted to find a female omega and start up a pack, he could find one online or something. But he hadn't been able to resist unloading it all. He'd told him he couldn't see himself breeding in the first place. Couldn't see himself with a woman, even. Couldn't see himself with a wolf.

The details he'd added just for the extra burn. He was bisexual, not gay. And it wasn't as if he could predict how he'd feel about every wolf he'd meet in the future. But with the emphasis on breeding that almost every wolf seemed to embody, finding an omega willing to mate with someone like him would be nearly impossible. The human world had moved forward where being gay was concerned, maybe because of all the extra babies around, but the shifter population was slow to progress. At least, certain shifter populations were. The cats, for example? They didn't seem to give a flying fuck about breeding. But they were solitary animals, and the humans loved them, so they could pretty much spend the full moon anywhere. Instead of going on runs in the woods like the wolves, they got to scamper about the suburbs, nothing to worry about except avoiding cars. Wolves, on the other hand, were big and ferocious, and the humans were ignorant and gun-wielding, and it was all just a pain in the ass.

He'd agreed to meet up with his former pack for the run this time, but only because his little sister Daisy had convinced him. She was only seventeen, and it was the least he could do when all the pressure about "strong local packs" would be falling on her now. Plus, he missed her.

But there were days before the full moon when his wolf was so close to the surface he hardly felt human. The most insignificant things would make him explode in anger, or consume him with lust.

It was nothing like the rut, which only happened once a year and was way heavier on the lust side of things, but it was still awful.

Now, he no longer had Carly to help channel his energy. He didn't have anyone for that. Thank God he'd met Heather at that cafe a couple months ago. At least her party would be a distraction. But right now? Right now, he wanted to chew into the whole world, and there wasn't anyone around to take his teeth.

He was curled up on his bed watching a movie on his phone when Lane texted him.

Hey

The house was dead quiet. Parker had worried Heather would be in her room, making noises that would trigger his lust, but she'd left early in the morning with a tired grin on her face. *"I'll be at Rina's,"* she'd said. Parker had given her his best effort at a smile. Truly, he was jealous.

But here Lane was, falling haphazardly into his lap.

All it took was that little *Hey* to trigger all kinds of images. Lane loose and warm under him, not frigid and scared. Forcing Lane down only to have him bare his throat in omega-like submission. But none of that would ever happen because Lane had rejected Parker's true form. Not his wolf, but that in-between state, when he still looked human but had claws, fangs, and orange eyes.

So why was Lane texting him? *What do you want?*

It took so long for Lane to answer that Parker thought he might not. Which would have been understandable. He *was* being hostile, but he didn't have it in him to fight the mood.

He was just getting back into the movie when Lane texted back.

Sorry if this is a bad time. Heather said something about the moon?

Parker narrowed his eyes at the screen. *What did she say?*

That I shouldn't go to her next party because you'll scare me

Parker barked a laugh. Suddenly he was the combustible combination of angry and amused. *She's right. I'd eat you up.*

Eat me up?

It's an expression. Mostly.

You said your fangs come out but you wouldn't hurt me

Parker breathed in and out slowly through his nose. It wouldn't take much to send his claws cutting out of his fingertips right now, and this conversation was rapidly going there. *I wouldn't.*

What if we met up now? Would you hurt me?

Parker hissed as his claws emerged. Very carefully, he texted, *Call me.* When Lane did, he said, "That's not happening. We can't."

"Okay. Do you still want to, though? You know... Hook up with me?"

Yes. God, yes. Parker's cock grew thick in his sweats. He only barely resisted the urge to give it some attention. But he didn't want to start breathing heavily, didn't want Lane to think him a creep. "Yeah."

"Could we talk about it? I know..." Lane breathed softly into the receiver. "I know this is a weird time for you, and if you happened to... God." He gave an awkward laugh. "Heather might be right about vamps being straightlaced."

Parker cinched his brows, trying to decipher the words. But, oh. *Oh.* "Do you want to have phone sex?"

"Um. We can do it over text if you want." Lane's words tumbled out too fast. "I used to sext guys all the time before I was turned. I mean, that was a long time ago, but—"

"Lane."

"Yeah?"

"You don't have to be nervous. I'll tell you what I'd do to you." Parker grinned at the sudden silence. His fangs grew longer, but with somewhere to focus his full-moon energy, he calmed. "Let's say you go to the party even though Heather warned you not to. I scent you as soon as you get there. You smell like blood."

"Oh, we're jumping right into it. Okay... I do?"

"Yes. But it's a subtle scent. Not like when a human bleeds." Parker closed his eyes and disappeared into the scene. He pictured the living room full of shifters, animalistic tension in the air. But he and Lane would go somewhere alone. Quiet. "We go to my room. I don't let anyone else talk to you because you're mine tonight. The other shifters can't be trusted. It's early, but they're already on edge, just like I am."

Lane's voice was quiet. "On edge how?"

"My wolf's pushing up against my skin, trying to get out. It can feel the moon. Tonight the moon's not quite full. I have all this pent-up energy that needs to get out, and I can either run, fight, or fuck. You and I are going to fuck." Parker listened for any protests. Had he been too straightforward so far? Would he be able to judge Lane's level of arousal, sexual or otherwise? "You'll tell me if I say something that freaks you out?"

"I guess. That wouldn't be very sexy, though."

"Yes it would. I'm an Alpha; I take care of you. I make you feel safe."

Lane let out a breath. "Okay. We're in your room."

"Yes. I close the door. Are you nervous?"

"Yeah. I don't want to bail on you again. You might stop being interested."

"No, I won't. I like a chase. Maybe you want to jerk off with me. No claws near you."

"No. I, uh...want you to walk me through it. Please, Parker."

The plea was like a punch to the gut, stiffening Parker's cock to full hardness. Didn't matter that Lane was only begging for information. "Do you have clothes on right now?"

"Yes," Lane hissed.

"What's wrong?"

"Fangs hurt."

"What's that mean?"

Lane laughed. "It means I want you."

Parker's knot filled in answer. "You have me. Get naked." Parker carefully shoved down his sweats while Lane obeyed.

"Okay," said Lane. "I'm naked."

Parker stroked himself slowly from the top of his knot to his leaking cockhead. He tried to focus more on the fantasy and less on the fact that Lane was a few miles away, naked because Parker had told him to be.

"I like foreplay. I want you begging for my knot when I give it to you. But at that party, I'm not in the mood. Can you take it?"

"I don't know."

"My claws are out. My teeth. But I won't hurt you with those. I might hurt you with my cock. Omegas get wet, but you don't."

"I'll prep myself. You don't have to worry about it. I come with my hole stretched and wet, but you'd better hurry. My body heals fast."

"Jesus, Lane."

Lane giggled softly, and Parker grinned again.

"I bend you over the bed. I fill your slick hole, and you can feel my knot bumping up against you." Parker stroked his cock in a vice grip, letting the edge of his fist bump up against his knot. "I rest my claws on the bed so I won't scratch you. I'm right up against your back, holding you down. Keeping you safe from every animal but me."

Lane's voice was full of breath. "You ever consider writing poetry, Parker? 'Cause damn."

Parker reserved all his poetry for situations like this, actually. "Are you touching yourself?"

"Yeah." His voice was strained.

"Fangs still hurting?"

"Yeah, I'm... Never mind."

Parker watched his forearm muscles flex as he stroked himself in a rhythm, coating his cock in precome. He made a lot more than most humans. "Tell me. I need honesty, or I can't help."

"You can't help. I'm thinking about blood. I'm wondering what yours would taste like. Probably—" He stopped to whimper. "Hotter than a human's."

Parker imagined Lane biting his neck and nearly growled into the phone. "You can't bite my neck. That's for mates. I'm fucking you from behind, so where can you bite me?"

"Wrist."

"All right. I fuck you hard. On each thrust, you feel my knot trying to edge inside of you. I give you my wrist. What do you do?"

"Hold it close. Kiss the vein..." He sounded so unsure. Parker wanted to ask questions, but instead, he waited patiently for Lane to keep going. "I bite you. It'll hurt. Is—Is that okay?"

"Yes." Parker imagined a mating bite. An omega staking their claim, but only with their Alpha's permission. It was all imagination because Parker had never allowed Carly to do it to him. "My knot pushes inside of you. It hurts at first, but you can take it, can't you?"

"Yes."

"Are you close, Lane?"

"Yes."

Parker opened his fist a little and encased his knot, squeezing as he imagined Lane's body would. It wasn't the same. He wished he had Lane here.

Lane moaned into his ear and then panted. "Parker."

"Did you come?"

"Yes. Please don't hang up yet."

The naked vulnerability exposed in Lane's voice hit Parker low in the stomach. "I can't. We're tied together, remember? My knot's getting bigger now." It was big already. Parker stroked himself off, grunting into the phone as come coated his fist and shot onto his stomach. He tried to pull his thoughts together, but for a few seconds, he could only breathe.

"How long do we stay together?"

"Ten minutes to a half hour."

They were both silent for a long while. Parker wanted to clean himself up, but he wasn't going to rush Lane. There were tissues by his bed; however, his claws would shred them if he tried to pull them out of the box.

"You know I can't come to the party," said Lane in a small voice.

"I know. Do you want to see each other after?"

"Yes. Just... Just text me."

CHAPTER THREE

"It was amazing." Heather's voice was breathy and low over the phone as she recounted the events of the party, which mostly involved her and Rina in their cat and mouse forms, chasing each other. That sounded scary to Lane, but Heather assured him they'd only partially shifted by the time she caught Rina.

Just now, it was midday after the night of the full moon. Lane could have gone to Heather's if he'd wanted, but it wasn't worth it. It only took ten minutes in the sun for him to get a wicked sunburn. The rest of the den was still sleeping, and Lane would have been sleeping, too, but he'd woken up from a dream about Theo. Now his heart was a rock, jagged and digging into the flesh surrounding it. Before calling Heather, he'd tried to reach Theo, since it was night where he was, but Theo hadn't answered. He was probably too busy. At least Lane had this barely extant thing with Parker to distract him.

"I'm glad you had a good time. Where's Rina now?"

"Home, I guess. I wanted her to stay longer, but... I don't know. She was a little closed off this morning."

"I'm sorry."

"It's fine. I'm sure I'm just being paranoid."

Lane turned onto his side in bed, staring into the curtained darkness. "Did you see Parker?"

"I did. But to be honest, I'm not comfortable telling you about it."

Lane's jagged heart grew spikes. He shouldn't have asked, had no right to care, either. He and Parker were far from together, and

Parker deserved to hook up with anyone who could handle it. "That's fine."

"I'm not trying to be rude. I just have to set some boundaries if I'm going to be the go-between for you two."

"Go-between? Did he talk about me?"

"He mentioned he spoke to you. But I should tell you wolves don't really do the whole hookup thing."

Lane's lips pulled back from his teeth as he tried not to get angry with her. "What are you talking about? You said Parker was going to hook up with someone at the party."

"That's a special case."

"A special case that happens monthly. And he tried to hook up with me too, remember?"

"Just listen."

Lane rolled his eyes but stayed silent.

"They don't do the hookup thing. The full moon and heat and rut stuff and whatnot is all biological, and Parker told me his wolf doesn't really like the premoon parties. He just does it to feel better. We have to channel our moon energy into something or we get violent. Humans will find out about us."

Lane could at least understand that last part. The main reason Theo had kept Lane confined to the den for two years was so he wouldn't lose control in public and make headlines. Then during that time, he'd had an escort for the same reason. If he happened to lose it now, Theo, Sam, and Erica would use their powers of enchantment to cover things up, but the repercussions for Lane would be bad. Theo might even disown him.

"So I won't hookup with him," said Lane.

"I didn't say that. He obviously likes you."

"Well, maybe I shouldn't. Maybe *he* shouldn't. You know I'm not ready for a boyfriend. I'll probably never be ready." One sexual encounter seemed damn near impossible on its own. A long-term thing? Parker wouldn't want to stick around once he knew how thick Lane's panic really was. Sometimes it seemed to dissipate, but then it would choke him seemingly out of nowhere.

"I know what happened to you was really awful, but eventually you have to move on from it. You're immortal now, Lane."

If Lane stayed in this conversation much longer, he was going to yell at her and stress himself out even more. "I have to go. Thanks for talking to me." *Thanks for picking up when Theo wouldn't.*

"You're welcome. Parker will be with his family for a couple days, but after that, I'm sure he'll text you. Okay?"

"Yeah, okay. Bye."

* * *

Lane's phone buzzed. He didn't answer it right away because he was feeding. He wasn't sexually attracted to women in the least, but he was presently preoccupied with the human straddling him. The ends of his prey's hair brushed his forearm as he gripped hard at her scalp, holding her still while he drank from her. He was practicing as much as he was fulfilling a need. He focused on her heartbeat against his lips and tongue. When it started to slow, he yanked his fangs out with a whine and pushed her away.

"Lane." That was Erica's stern voice. "Easy."

The human toppled dizzily to the floor.

"I'm sorry," said Lane. "It hurts to stop." His jaw throbbed. All his senses were still focused on the human at his feet, and on the fact that he hadn't killed her. There was more warm nectar to suck, and he longed to hear her heartbeat speed and then fade, longed to feel her go limp and lifeless in his arms. He drew his knees up to his chest and hid his face, groaning.

"Breathe," said Erica. The human was getting up, a dazed little whimper leaving her lips. "Just breathe." To Lane's prey, she said, "Go to the kitchen, sweetheart. Eat something."

Lane latched onto the prey's heartbeat and listened to it even as she disappeared into the other part of the house.

"Lane," said Erica again, and he lost track of the weakened thudding.

"What?" His own heart was going fast and hard.

"You did well. You're getting better."

"It *hurts.*" Let them call him dramatic, he didn't care. It was like his whole face was a throbbing bruise, with most of the pain centered in his jawline. And his skin was growing warmer and warmer. If he got any hotter, he'd start sweating blood. He listened to Erica and forced himself to breathe.

While he was gasping, he felt his phone buzz against his hip for a second time. This time he reached for it, fingers shaking as he opened the screen and squinted at its brightness. The den was dark—protected by the blackout drapes the human servants had drawn earlier—and Lane's pupils were fully dilated.

Hey

Come over.

Following the second text was an address.

Amazing. Parker *would* get back to him at the worst possible time. Hissing around his still-exposed fangs, Lane sped away from the living room. Now that he'd lost track of his prey's heartbeat, varied thumps came together as an echo over everything. Mercifully, the hallway off the foyer only had a few distinct heartbeats. One of them, a human's, was beating very fast, but it was a heavy sound. This one was excited, not dying.

He called Parker.

"Hello?"

"Hey. I can't."

"Why not?"

"I'm..." If it were another vamp, he would have said he was hungry. "...vamped out."

"Huh?"

"I'm still new at feeding, and one of my elders was coaching me, and I can't—I can't turn it off sometimes. If I come over, I could hurt you."

"You won't hurt me."

"Yeah, I will."

"I'm an Alpha, and you're a babyvamp."

Lane hissed involuntarily. "Don't call me that."

"Fine. You're a young vampire. I'm stronger, I promise. Let me pick you up."

The thought of a shifter driving up to a den full of feeding vamps was laughable. The thought of Erica or Sam—and by extension, Theo—finding out about Parker wasn't funny at all. "No."

"Why not?"

"It's gated. Plus, my elders would freak. They barely tolerate Heather, and if they figure out I'm—" He thought it over. Seeing, dating... None of it was accurate. "There's no way you're coming here."

Parker huffed into the phone. "But I really want to see you again."

It wasn't a real thing he meant. It was like what strangers said to keep you going while you sucked their dicks. *That mouth. You're so sexy.* Even though Lane hadn't been with anyone in a while, memories from his various sexual encounters were still clear in his undead brain.

"Sorry," he said bitterly.

"How long till you aren't 'vamped out' anymore?"

"Um... Couple of hours?"

"Come over then."

"It'll be too late."

"It'll be four in the morning."

Lane ran his tongue over his fangs, relishing the taste of human blood that still lingered. He wanted more. "I'd have to stay all day if I did that. I won't race home when we're done hanging out and risk my safety to beat the sunlight."

Parker answered too quickly, "That's fine."

Lane really should have said no.

But he actually said, "All right then," and immediately went to work trying to bury his fangs.

* * *

Hopefully Lane hadn't picked up on Parker's desperation. His wolf was a hot mess. Running under the moon last night with his disappointed family hadn't even begun to uncoil the knots of tension that came from being in human form almost all the time. On top of that was everything his human brain had been feeding his wolf about pack expectations, and not being Alpha enough, and dumping Carly. He felt like shit. And he needed a distraction, one that could drive it all away.

Lane was that distraction. Lane had wounds that Parker could soothe in return.

It was almost five before he showed up. Lane looked like shit, too. His fangs were out, resting against his bottom lip, and his pupils were swallowing his irises. He looked calm otherwise, but his heart was beating faintly, and when he spoke, his voice was gravelly. "I couldn't get them to go back in."

Parker felt highly unqualified to deal with that. He'd lusted after vampires, but he'd only ever gotten as far as first base with one. And it had been a stranger, not someone he could ask questions of like he'd been doing with Lane. But he would do his best like he did with everything. He would take care of it.

Seeing Lane in person after that phone call was...intense. Parker reached for his hand and pulled him inside, taking him through the living room, into the hallway, into his room. He closed the door just as he'd said he would. Except there were no guests in the house, and Heather was asleep.

Parker went to sit on the bed. He was shirtless, dressed in a pair of low-hanging sweatpants, but Lane seemed impervious. His big-pupiled eyes were darting over the room, like he was scanning for threats. Parker held out a hand to him. "Hey. Come here."

Those eyes snapped onto Parker. "I'm scared."

Lane's fear hardened his cock; he ought to have felt some guilt for that. But he wanted to pull Lane close and cradle him and take that fear away. "I know. C'mere."

Lane toed off his white Chuck Taylors and came to sit on the bed with a leg bent under him and his jacket still on. There was about an inch between Lane's bent knee and Parker's leg.

Parker took a moment to just observe Lane—his skin, upon closer inspection, tinted pink and his high cheekbones and smooth jaw. "Can you kiss with fangs?" he asked, pitching his voice low so as not to startle.

Lane looked down at his lap. "I think so. I haven't kissed anyone since I was turned."

"How long has that been?"

Lane's heart beat a little harder, and his cheeks grew pinker. "Two years and three months. It's not that long to a vampire. I have forever."

Parker smiled. Yes, Lane had forever, but he'd only just been turned. Had time started moving faster to him already? "Would you mind if I kiss you?"

"I might nick you accidentally."

"That's all right."

Lane looked up at him with wide eyes, but he nodded. "Okay."

Parker turned toward him and touched him under the chin. His fangs were so cute. Just two of them, almost as small as human teeth. He rubbed over Lane's bottom lip with his thumb and then gently nudged one of his fangs.

Lane's whole body shuddered.

"You like that?"

"Yeah."

Parker couldn't keep the smile from his mouth as he leaned in to kiss Lane. Just a quick peck at first. When Lane parted his lips, Parker gave him tongue, making sure to slide the muscle along each fang. Lane moaned and came closer, settling a hand on Parker's bare side. Lane was human temperature now, not quite as hot as Parker.

Lane tried to take the lead. Parker gripped him at the back of the neck as he would an overzealous omega, but the gesture didn't work on Lane. Parker tried to meet him, kissed him more vigorously. He was still managing to keep his fangs at bay, so he bit Lane's bottom lip.

Then Lane did nick him.

Parker had only a second to register the pain before Lane pulled back, unhinged his jaw, and buried his fangs in Parker's throat.

Theoretically, he could have made him stop. He could have pried open his mouth and forced him off. But the sensation was somewhere between pain and debilitating pleasure. Wolves were sensitive at the neck, and this was where Parker's mate would have bitten him.

His wolf reacted, making him painfully hard, swelling his knot, and pushing his fangs and claws out through his skin. He toppled backward onto the bed at an angle, one leg dangling off and the other bent, his bare foot against the comforter. He had claws out of his toes, too.

Lane didn't seem to notice Parker's fangs as he fell forward to straddle him, his own fangs still embedded in Parker's neck. He moaned against the wound. He was apparently attempting to hold Parker by the hair, but it was cut too short, so Lane's palm simply cradled Parker's skull, rubbing a little over the buzzed, blond strands.

Parker's body went soft everywhere except where it counted. His cock was trapped against the fleece-lined fabric of his sweats and Lane's hips on top of his own.

Eventually, Lane took his teeth out. He seemed to come back to himself, though his eyes were hooded and his face flushed. "Oh

God." He clamped a hand over Parker's wound. "I'm sorry. You said not to bite you there."

Parker struggled to get the words out past his arousal. "I know. It's okay."

"I can't heal you." Lane blinked slowly, as though he could barely lift his lids. "Drank too much. Sleepy..."

Parker didn't know exactly what healing him entailed. But he'd heal naturally in a few hours. Lane collapsed on top of him, his face hidden against the uninjured side of Parker's neck, his hand still over the bite. Parker lay there, keeping his claws to himself. Soon the pressure on his wound lessened; apparently, Lane had fallen asleep.

Parker looked up at the ceiling. He took deep, slow breaths. Eventually, his claws would go back in, and his cock would go soft again. Maybe then he'd be mad at Lane for going against what he'd said about biting his neck. But he probably wouldn't be.

* * *

As Lane got ready to head back to the den, Parker acted like everything was fine. He kissed Lane good-bye on the top of the head, but Lane had trouble returning the affection. He couldn't believe he was wrong for Parker in yet another way. Couldn't control his damage. Couldn't control his hunger.

He was hoping he could steal upstairs as soon as he got to the den. He needed to change out of his jacket and shirt, both of which were stained with Parker's blood. But he'd managed to avoid his denmates' ire too many times already. His luck had run out.

"Where have *you* been?" Erica was on him as soon as he entered the foyer. She was impeccably dressed as always, her dark hair glossy. Her eyes zeroed in on the bloodstains and widened.

"I went to see a friend," said Lane carefully.

"What friend?"

"His name is Parker."

"Human or vampire?" Erica sniffed, obviously trying to scent the blood. She took a step closer and shifted her gaze to Lane's.

She tended to be softer on him than Theo and Sam, but Lane still found her unblinking stare unnerving. "Werewolf. Don't worry, I hurt him more than he hurt me."

"I wasn't aware you knew any werewolves."

"Just one." Lane wrapped his arms around himself and broke the eye contact.

"Is he safe?"

"Seems to be." Lane just knew she'd tell Theo about this. Even if he got angry, it would be worth it for the call. At least Lane hoped he'd call.

"Okay." Erica put one of her long-nailed hands against the back of Lane's neck and kissed him on the head, just like Parker had done. "Be careful."

"I will." He knew the risks. He hadn't been drained to death just to learn nothing. But secretly, he hoped Theo would order him not to see Parker. Then he wouldn't have to worry about it anymore. He wouldn't have to try to control himself, wouldn't have to make himself into someone who could be with Parker or anyone else.

Not even two hours later, Lane's phone rang. When he saw Theo's name on the screen, medium-sized and innocent looking in the Android system font, his heart began pumping. He hesitated only a moment before picking up.

"Hello?"

"Hello, my child. I believe there's something we need to discuss."

CHAPTER FOUR

At least Lane hadn't run off this time. That was Parker's only consolation as he overanalyzed the day they'd spent together, his conclusion being that he'd completely lost control. Not only had he allowed Lane to bite him in his most sensitive place, he'd also lain there passively while Lane had used him to sate himself. It wasn't the dynamic Parker preferred. And yet he couldn't stop thinking about it. His wolf longed to sink its teeth into Lane in return, to mark him as Parker's and show him his place.

Really, he was lucky to be starting his new job the following night at Meta, a shifter bar in downtown Royal Oak. But his sour mood hadn't cleared up, and on the ride over together, Heather, who worked a second job there as a waitress, must have picked up on it.

"You might think people just tip every bartender, but they don't. You have to smile and chat and stuff."

"I'm not an idiot. I know the job description."

"I'm just saying."

He put on his best Alpha smile when they got there, though. Plus, a dumbass could pour shots, and that was all shifters ever ordered. Considering most of them were probably young professionals who had to keep their beastliness in check eight hours a day, Parker couldn't blame them for wanting to get as drunk as possible. The tips they gave him were adequate. He hadn't made any glaring mistakes. Still, by the time he and Heather left, his mood had spoiled even further.

He scowled and shoved his hands into his pockets as they made their way to the parking garage.

"What's up with you?" asked Heather.

"Nothing's 'up.'"

"It obviously is. Does it have to do with Lane?"

"No."

Heather raised her brows like she didn't believe him. They found the car, and she pulled out into the deserted three a.m. streets of the usually bustling downtown suburb.

"Okay, it is about Lane. He bit me. Here." Heather glanced over as Parker tipped his head back and ran his fingers over the spot where Lane had sunk his fangs. He shivered with the touch. "Normally, that's a mating ritual thing."

Heather laughed. It was an awkward, nervous sound; otherwise, Parker might have bitten her head off. "Shit. You're not like, bonded, are you?"

Parker rolled his eyes. "No. We haven't even had sex yet."

"Just checking."

They rode in silence after that, which was fine with Parker, but when they were almost home, Heather spoke again. "You shouldn't have let him do that."

"Excuse me?" The defensive anger that flooded him was irrational, but he didn't try to stop it. Alphas weren't supposed to like it when people told them what they should or shouldn't do.

"I don't know... What if he sees you as food now?"

"Since when are you some vampire expert?"

Leaves and gravel crunched under the car tires as Heather pulled into their back driveway.

"I'm not. I didn't even know vampires could feed from shifters. I mean, is that safe for Lane?"

Parker tasted blood as his fangs extended. "He was *fine*." As soon as Heather shut off the car, he flung his door open. But he had to wait for her to let him into the house. He'd been living here for almost a month, but she hadn't made him a key yet. Here was another way Parker was submitting. To a *house cat*.

Once inside, he went headed for the kitchen. Heather did too, and opened the fridge for her Lactaid. She always went straight for it as soon as she got off work. Parker went for the vodka. He'd had a few shots on the job, but they hadn't touched him. Hot werewolf blood burned the liquor away too fast.

"Are you okay?" asked Heather, unscrewing the cap on the carton. "I didn't mean to piss you off—"

"I'm fine. Lane's fine. Everything's fine." Parker didn't bother pouring the vodka into a glass, just took the bottle with him to his room. He took out his phone; he knew Lane would be awake, and he wasn't going to sit and stew about all the mistakes he may or may not have committed.

Should I have stopped you from biting me? Is shifter blood healthy for you? No sense beating around the bush, he figured.

Except Lane didn't answer for like an hour, and by the time he did, the bottle of vodka was nearly empty, and Parker was copping a healthy buzz.

Yeah, I think so. I fell asleep because I was full

Unfortunately, that didn't make Parker feel any better. *Cool,* he texted back.

Are we playing 20 questions? Is it my turn now?

Parker laughed bitterly and took the last swig. *Shoot.*

Have you ever accidentally hurt somebody?

Weren't people supposed to ask lighter things during twenty questions? What's your favorite color, maybe? *Have I broken someone's heart? Yeah.* That was exactly what he'd done with Carly. He dropped the vodka bottle into his bedside trash and leaned his head back.

No. Physically

"Fuck," Parker muttered. Of course Lane was asking about physical pain. Always with the fear of Parker's claws. Normally, he'd be fine with walking Lane through it all one more time, but after tonight...

Pass. Next question.

It's your turn then

Parker smirked. *Do you like me?*

The answer didn't come for a while. *Sure*

Smooth.

What do you want me to say?

Nothing. It doesn't matter.

Are you okay? What's this about?

It was about Parker being the stereotypically pushy Alpha who pressured people into relationships before it was time. He'd just met him. Shifters jumped into relationships all the time, but did vampires? Since they were immortal, Parker couldn't see it. *Just don't bite me on my neck again.*

I told you I was sorry

I know.

Do you like me?

Parker had asked the question first, but reading it now made it feel like they were on the playground, or in class passing notes.

Yes.

Then answer the question you passed on earlier. I'm in trouble with my Maker because I spent time alone with you but didn't tell any of my elders first. They say shifters are dangerous. So are you?

Parker furrowed his brow and tried his best, both to answer and to not get offended. *I would never hurt you on purpose. I'm sorry I got you in trouble.*

You're strong enough to rip my head off. You could kill me

Not by accident. That requires effort. And I don't go around tearing off vamp heads. Believe me.

What if something bad happened between us and you were angry?

I'm not a fucking murderer? No offense but your Maker sounds prejudiced.

He isn't.

Parker had noticed Lane didn't usually end texts with a period. This one was like a bullet hole.

Okay. But you don't have to worry.

Fine

Talking to Lane was a nightmare, in person and through texts. But still, Parker didn't want to give up on this. Maybe it was stubbornness. Maybe it was what he'd told Lane: he liked the chase. But could he handle it for much longer? Maybe someone else would be better at dealing with Lane's fears and problems.

But Alphas fixed problems.

Look, I'm a little drunk. So I'm going to go to bed, okay?

Ok. Sweet dreams. I'm sorry

Parker groaned at the apology, switched off his phone, and buried his face in his pillow.

* * *

Lane almost didn't go to the next shifter party at Heather's. Theo hadn't forbidden him from going, but his disapproving tone was still fresh in Lane's ears, and things with Parker were...off. After texting with him a few nights before, Lane felt even worse about not keeping his fangs to himself. He wasn't sure if Parker wanted to see him. Part of him hoped he wouldn't be at the party, even if he were still staying at Heather's.

Lane had tried to talk to Heather about Parker, but she hadn't been very receptive. When Lane got to the party, she had a hard, faraway look in her eyes, so Lane didn't try to talk about Parker then either.

"What's up with you?" he asked, sliding his fingers into the back pockets of his skinny jeans and trying to look inconspicuous as he glanced around the living room for Parker. Lane didn't see his beanie or buzzed head anywhere.

"Rina's avoiding me. I'm sure it's nothing."

"I thought things were going well with you guys. Is she going to be here?"

"I don't know." Heather threw up her hands. Lane grimaced and was about to sit down next to her on the couch when she got up suddenly. "Will you do some shots with me?"

"Sure."

He followed her into the kitchen but declined the tequila she offered. To him, it was just salt on fire, and it never went down smooth. He searched the cabinets for vodka but didn't find any.

"Hey."

Parker.

Lane's fingers froze on a cabinet handle.

Heather set her shot glass down, raised her brows bitterly, and said, "You know what? Catch ya later."

Lane gave her a sympathetic look as she left. He knew he should tell Parker he'd catch up with him some other time, that he should keep Heather company while she worried about her situation with Rina. But he couldn't bring himself to do that with Parker right here.

He closed the cabinet, turned around to lean back against a counter, and curled his hands around the edge of its granite top. "Hey."

Parker fixed him with an invasive, serious gaze. The attention would have made Lane blush if his body had been excited enough, but he just stared back, gripping the countertop hard and scratching his nails against its underside. Maybe Parker did want to see him.

"Looking for this?" Parker produced a half-finished fifth of peach vodka and came close enough to touch the bottle to Lane's stomach.

"Yeah," Lane said.

"You know, it wouldn't kill you to bring your own liquor instead of always filching ours." He could have been teasing, except his expression stayed slack and his tone serious.

"Sorry."

"Are you?" Parker leaned in, squeezing the bottle between them, and slid his nose against Lane's.

"Not really." As he spoke, his mouth was very nearly against Parker's. The closeness alone made his chest stiffen. In a moment or two, his heart would start beating, but he was still cold. He hadn't fed for nearly twenty-four hours.

Parker pushed the bottle downward, until it slid against Lane's groin. The sensation was somewhere between unpleasant and pleasantly stimulating, which made Lane turn his head.

"No, don't do that." Parker gripped Lane's jaw with his free hand and turned his head back around. "Don't avoid my kiss like it's gonna hurt you."

"I didn't know you were gonna—"

Parker cut him off with his mouth. The sheer heat of Parker's skin and tongue whited out everything else. Parker set the bottle on the counter and pressed closer, and Lane's heart began beating. His fangs clicked out and connected with the flesh of Parker's lip.

"Shit." Parker pulled back but kept their lower halves pressed together. He touched a finger to his mouth where there was now a smear of blood.

Lane fixed on that; his jaw throbbed painfully. He sniffed with his nostrils flared.

"You're a little monster, you know that?" said Parker.

Lane's gaze flicked up. "You turned me on."

"I can see that."

"Well?" The pain of hunger made him irritable. He shoved at Parker's waist. "Take me somewhere." *Let's actually fuck this time.*

Parker responded by pressing Lane harder against the counter, until the granite dug painfully into his back. But Parker was a warm, yielding pressure against his front, and he rubbed their hardening cocks together.

"But I've got you right here," Parker whispered. "And this is my house."

What did it matter? The shifters would hear everything no matter what. At least they weren't in the living room, fucking on the floor like the vampire guests at the den did sometimes. When Parker moved to unfasten Lane's jeans, Lane rested his hands on Parker's shoulders and looked down between them.

"You're gonna be dry, aren't you?" Lane didn't grasp the meaning of the words until Parker had his cock free, exposing the bloody precome at the tip. "Shit, guess not."

"Blood replaces all fluids," Lane explained calmly. Including saliva, so the inside of Lane's mouth was perpetually tinted red. If Parker had noticed before, he hadn't mentioned it.

Parker undid his own pants. For a second, Lane was distracted by the muscles in his forearms, but then his eyes fell on his knot. *Too big,* said his instincts, but they would have said that without the knot, considering his cock on its own was gigantic.

Parker reached for one of Lane's hands and guided him down toward it, until Lane was wrapping his fingers around the shaft just above the knot. Immediately, precome dripped from the head.

"Your hand's cold." Parker groaned at the sensation.

"I'm warming up."

"Shh. Just stroke it."

Being shushed and ordered in one breath had Lane all too ready to comply. This was an Alpha wolf, he remembered suddenly. Lane was not the one in charge.

He did as he was told, and even tried to wrap his hand around the knot, but it was too big to hold all at once. Still, Parker's shaft became soaked, so Lane must have been doing okay.

After a few minutes, Parker shoved Lane's fingers away and gripped both of their cocks in one big hand, stroking fast. Lane pitched forward into Parker's upper body, stiffening when the urge to bite nearly overtook him. "Parker, I—"

"Shut up."

Lane whined. He bit into his lip and blood poured onto Parker's shoulder.

Parker must not have noticed, because he kept going with his hand, and Lane's body temperature rose and rose, until his skin was flushed all over.

When Lane came, spurts of blood dribbled onto Parker's fingers, and then the knot at the base of Parker's cock was contracting, and several times the amount of come Lane had ever seen from humans shot out the tip. The mess between them was sticky and pink, and the scent of Parker's spunk filled Lane's nostrils. He pulled back and wiped at his chin, whining at the overwhelming nature of it all. He was slow moving and postorgasmic, but his jaw still throbbed. He felt feverish.

Parker looked dazed. "Okay," he said. He took his hand away and cleaned them up with paper towels from a roll above the sink. He pulled up his sweats and tried to do the same with Lane's pants, but Lane snapped to alertness and swatted him away. He yanked up his jeans and looked around them. Empty kitchen. Voices mingling together in the living room. No one had disturbed them, probably because they could hear it all and knew to steer clear.

"You're a fucking mess," said Parker. There was a pleased gleam in his eye as he went to grip Lane's jaw and inspect his healed but bloody lip and chin.

Lane swatted at him again. "Get the fuck off of me."

"What the hell's wrong with you?"

"I'm hungry." Lane fought the urge to hiss. Parker's heartbeat was like a punch to the temples every time it sounded.

"Maybe if you stop bitching, I'll take you to my room and give you a drink."

Lane fixed his hair. "I assumed you wouldn't want to."

"You bite me when I let you. That's the deal. Don't assume things."

"Fine."

"Fine."

Parker grabbed for Lane yet again, and Lane once more swatted. But Parker seemed set on steering his body for him. He circled his big fingers around Lane's wrist and yanked him out of the kitchen, to the hallway, and into his room.

"You're so fucking—" *handsy,* Lane was going to say. But his words ended in a groan against flesh as Parker pressed his wrist to Lane's lips, shoving him so hard against the door that his skull made an audible thud against it.

Parker petted back through Lane's hair. He cupped his cranium and seemed to check for injury. But Lane wouldn't have minded a temporary concussion, not if that was the price for blood like this. So hot. So sweet. So filling. Even without the human blood pregame he'd had before seeing Parker the last time, Parker's wolf blood sated Lane, until his lashes were fluttering down over his eyes, and Parker was catching him as he fell forward against his torso, fangs sheathed.

"There we go," said Parker in a soft, husky voice as he carried Lane's limp form to the bed. "Now you're manageable."

Lane was barely conscious, but he still caught the insult. "Eat me," he muttered.

Parker laughed.

* * *

Lane came back to consciousness slowly, cocooned in warmth. Parker's well-shaped arms were wrapped around him, his chest pressed to Lane's spine, his warm breath caressing the top of Lane's head. When Lane moved a little, Parker did, too. He squeezed Lane with his arms and then relaxed again.

"Enjoy your nap?"

"Mhm." Lane would have liked to stay here forever. When had anyone held him like this? He couldn't remember. Adrian hadn't, and though Theo had held him a few times, it was different. Face-to-face with just their hands gripping, their foreheads touching. Platonic somehow. Lane had sometimes wished he'd do it like this, but Theo had done it just to satisfy the Bond, and the touching had grown lighter and lighter since the change. Now, Lane was lucky to get a pat on the back every once in a while. Lane would be lucky just to have his Maker in the same house again, in the same city.

Parker wasn't afraid of touching. He didn't even make Lane ask for it.

"You're so warm all the time," Lane said, and turned in Parker's arms. He looked at Parker's brown eyes and touched his strong nose and stubbled jaw.

"Do you like that about me?" asked Parker.

"I don't know." Part of him would have liked another cold body by his side. "I miss my Maker."

"That's the one who turned you?"

"Yeah. He's away on a trip."

A crease appeared in Parker's brow. "Are you two together?"

"No. He saved my life. Now he's off at a conference, and he doesn't call. Except when he found out I was seeing a shifter."

"You told him about me?"

"No, I told Erica. She's another one of my denmates. Or they're my elders, technically, since I'm the youngest in the den. I spent all day out with you, which is unusual for me, and I don't like lying to them." Lane traced each of Parker's eyebrows and the lines in his forehead. "I won't let them stop me from seeing you, though."

Parker stilled Lane's hand with his own. "Will they try that?"

"I don't think so."

"If they do, you can come here. Stay with me." The weight of Parker's gaze seemed to land in Lane's chest. Surely his elders wouldn't leave him like that. But then, Theo had. He imagined being without Erica to help him feed and nearly sent his own heart beating.

"Okay," he said.

"I'm serious."

"Okay." Lane took Parker's hand in his and stroked a thumb over the bite wound he'd left earlier. "Would you like me to heal this for you?" He was pretty sure he could bring his fangs out now that he'd slept a little. And maybe he could even put them back in on his own since he'd been sated.

"How's that work anyway?"

"I bite myself and spread some of my blood on it."

"No thanks."

"It's not a big deal." Lane ducked his head to kiss the wound, holding Parker's gaze. Parker's cheeks darkened. Lane longed to give him a fresh bite even if he wasn't hungry.

"It's fine," said Parker. "Do you want to rejoin the party? Mingle and stuff?"

"No. I like this."

"Good." Parker hooked his leg around Lane. "I want you to stay here forever."

So they'd had the same thought. Like when both Lane and Theo wanted to touch to make the Bond-induced stress of separation go away, but they always seemed to put it off. It always hurt. This, though, with Parker, didn't.

Chapter Five

Lane let Parker kiss him good-bye. And it felt good, like foreplay, but he had to go. Even if Parker was adorable when he was half-asleep, stumbling just before he pressed Lane to the wall, his eyes heavy-lidded as he stared at him and rubbed both his ears.

"Stop," Lane said, laughing.

Parker smiled. He gave Lane a last, quick peck.

Outside, Lane turned on his phone and texted Erica. *On my way home.* That was part of the agreement he and Theo had reached. Of course, it had only come after a tiresome, endless lecture about long-time friction between vampires and shifters, and why it had always been this way. *"I will not attempt to dissuade you from exploration, child, but you will settle my nerves by keeping us informed."* Lane was helpless to argue against an admission like that; Theo cared about him. Lane wondered if it was only the Bond, and why most times, he couldn't feel Theo's affection.

When Lane walked into the foyer, Erica was on him, speeding from the house's depths to come inspect him. She touched his jaw gently with her burgundy nails and turned his face side-to-side as if she was looking for wounds, even though anything like that would have already healed. Lane had washed off Parker's blood where it had dried on his chin, had even gargled some of Parker's mouthwash to remove the scent.

"Everything go okay?" she said.

Field notes, Hookup #1: Werewolf dicks are wild. "It was just a party."

Erica patted him on the cheek before letting him go. "Your eyes are still dilated, sweetheart." Then she turned and headed out of the foyer.

What did that mean? Had she guessed that Lane had had sex with Parker, or liked him, or had fed on him? He didn't mind his elders knowing about the former two so much, but the latter, he would keep secret. Theo hadn't mentioned anything about Lane feeding on Parker, whether it was all right for him to do so, or to get that full or not. Maybe he didn't know. Maybe Theo hadn't mentioned it because he didn't want Lane wondering about the taste of shifter. Because Lane had never felt like that on human blood. He figured it would take more than a humanful to get there. Perhaps a small massacre, perhaps a regular-sized one. And it would never be so hot, even if the prey were scared and running or helplessly aroused. Lane wasn't sure he'd want human blood ever again, actually.

This realization hit him at the top of the stairs. He paused and looked down at his white shoes, worn but still stark against the dark red carpet, and he thought this could all go terribly wrong. Never mind the risk to his heart. Never mind the risk of getting close to another guy with fangs, which would inevitably bring everything back. How he'd trusted the wrong vampire. How he'd gotten to that lovely, dizzy place that came with feeding. But Adrian hadn't stopped when he was supposed to. He'd taken all of Lane's blood. Lane had tried to tell him, had gripped the fabric of Adrian's hoodie with weak fingers, but Lane had still ended up slipping away toward God.

Instead of God, he'd met Theo, who wasn't nearly as fallible. *"You're safe, you're safe. Just drink, human."*

No wonder Lane's denmates were worried about him.

In his room, trying to put his mind on other things, he sent Heather a text. *Hey sorry I disappeared. Did you work things out with Rina?* But even after a couple of hours had passed, she hadn't answered him. Maybe she and Rina were making up. Obviously, if they were busy kissing, Heather wouldn't be able to text.

* * *

Parker was busy. It was a Saturday, and Meta was stuffed, and there was a gigantic bear with two similarly gigantic friends behind him who'd ordered sixteen shots of four different liquors. They were going to run out of shot glasses at this rate, and in Parker's opinion, the rat who was washing them needed to go a little fucking faster. There were *tips* at stake.

Let me come over

Parker had just enough time to read the message; he couldn't *not* read a message from Lane. Taking orders and bitching at the rat took only about twenty-five percent of his mental effort, so with the rest of it, he formulated his response.

An hour later, on his smoke break, he messaged Lane back one-handed.

Are you seriously giving orders to an Alpha? I'm at work.

Lane answered in under a minute. *How much longer?*

Three more hours.

I'll wait

Worry tensed the muscles along Parker's back. *You okay?*

No, but it's not an emergency. Just need to see you

It took everything for Parker to pocket his phone and go back to work.

At the end of the night, he sent Lane a text to let him know he was on his way home. But when he got there, Heather met him at the door and said Lane had been waiting inside for forty-five minutes.

She whispered, "He's all—" and opened her fingers in front of her eyes. Vamped-out, Parker figured.

"I'm sorry." They walked through the kitchen together. "I know you were trying to chill tonight." It was one of Heather's rare nights off. Her blonde waves were up in a messy bun, and her curvy body was lost in loose pajamas.

"Yeah, well, we watched an episode of *Charmed*," she said.

Parker already owed a lot to Heather—the job and the room and everything—but he gained even more respect for her as a result of this. If he'd been living at his parents' house and his vampire lover had shown up there, he would have been sent away or worse.

Lane was sitting on the couch with his knees drawn up against his chest.

"Hey," said Parker cautiously, moving toward him. The freeze frame on the television was of a redheaded Rose McGowan. Heather stood to the side with her arms crossed.

"Hey." Lane looked up with his big eyes.

"You wanna come to my room, maybe?" asked Parker.

Lane nodded. He stood, and with his knees no longer shadowing his face, the points of his fangs were now visible. Parker held out a hand, and Lane slid his fingers into it. Parker got the sense he was suddenly dealing with a little kid. But it wasn't exactly like that. Lane was acting like an omega wolf, pouting with eyes glowing and fangs out, like Carly used to do before her heats. Parker hadn't been allowed to have her then. They hadn't wanted cubs.

Parker gave Heather a smile and mouthed "Thank you" when Lane looked away. Once they were in his room and he'd closed the door, Lane came close. He wasn't monstrous like usual, didn't hiss or claw. He just nuzzled Parker's nose with his.

"I should take a shower," Parker said. Despite the continuously dropping temperature outside, Parker's T-shirt was damp and clinging to him at the base of his spine. Closing up a bar on Saturday was hard work.

Lane said, "No. Don't." It was as if he wanted to be wrapped in Parker's scent—if vampires even thought like that.

Parker took him to the bed. He gently lifted him and lay him down. "What's got you all fangy, hmm?" He crawled on top of him.

"I had a dream." Lane's heartbeat was thudding gently, and he was lukewarm. He touched Parker's face and watched him with nervous eyes as Parker hovered over him.

"What kind of dream?"

"Bad memories kind."

"Oh." Parker didn't have memories bad enough to dream about. Almost always he dreamed from his wolf's perspective, of woods blurring past and his paws thumping earth. "Do you want to tell me about it?"

Lane shook his head.

"Did you come for sex?"

"If you want."

Parker frowned.

Lane's expression sharpened. "Don't look at me like that."

"Like what?"

"Like I'm weird for saying that."

"I just don't think we're at the stage where you can say 'if you want,' and I can get a hard-on."

Lane cinched his brows angrily and jutted out his bottom lip.

Adorable.

Parker laughed and dropped down on top of him. He slid a hand over his cheek and touched that pouting set of lips with his thumb. "Did you come for my blood?"

Lane didn't answer.

"You did, didn't you?"

"If you want," he said. "If you don't want, then no. I'm not hungry."

Parker slid the pad of his thumb along a fang.

Lane flinched, but he didn't protest. He moved his fingers to rest over Parker's forearm.

They locked eyes. "Feel good?" Parker asked.

Lane nodded.

Parker slid his thumb up farther, until he was massaging the gum around the base of the fang. Lane made a pained sound and dropped his brows together, so Parker moved his thumb to the other side and did the same thing there.

Lane's nails dug into his forearm. "Hurts," he said.

Parker took his hand away.

"No. More, please."

Parker wanted to give him more. He wanted so badly to do that. But Lane's show of submission had his wolf waking up and his claws coming out. "Man..."

"What?"

"You can't say stuff like that." Parker trailed the tips of his claws down Lane's face, earning him a shiver. Lane's heartbeat spiked, but he didn't seem afraid...

"Why not? It's called communicating." Lane dipped his chin, giving Parker a serious look.

Parker wiggled his claws in front of Lane's face. "Now I can't massage your fangs until you're begging to bite me."

Lane rolled his eyes. "Do it with your tongue then." Like Parker was completely stupid for not thinking of that.

"And what if my fangs come out while I'm kissing you?"

Lane gave the middle distance an impatient glare. "They didn't come out last time you kissed me."

"You weren't like this last time."

He speared Parker with that same glare. "Like what?"

Parker's voice got deeper as arousal rushed through him. "Needy." He slid down Lane's body and hid his face against his stomach. His fangs grew in his mouth, but he didn't want Lane to run from him again.

"Parker?" Lane's fingers were featherlight against Parker's head.

"Sorry. Fangs."

Lane's heartbeat grew stronger, faster. "Show me."

"I can shift them back. Just give me a minute."

"No. It's okay. Please."

Parker slowly lifted his head, mouth hanging open.

Lane's eyes widened, and he tensed. But he didn't move. He didn't run. "Why are they out now and not before? I'm confused."

Parker huffed a laugh. "I want you."

"More than last time?"

"Yes." His cock was hard, probably leaking in his boxers. "You were upset. You came to me. Like an omega to their Alpha. I...like being needed."

Lane gave him a heavy look. "Oh. If we..." Lane's skin was getting pinker by the minute, and he looked past Parker's shoulder. "If we have sex, will you hurt me?"

"I can control myself. I might scratch you a little accidentally, but I'll be as careful as I can." Probably he should have reassured him that they didn't need to have sex. Parker could control himself in that aspect, too. But he didn't want to.

"Okay." Lane dropped his arms back against the pillows above his head and went limp. "Do what you want to me."

Parker grinned and melted at the same time. He pulled back and ripped off his T-shirt, scratching himself in the process.

Lane's nostrils flared.

"You're going to have to take off your clothes first, babe," said Parker.

"You can take them off."

"I'll rip them. What would your elders say?"

"You're right," Lane grumbled. His limbs turned to blurs as he undressed in just a few seconds.

Parker mirrored him, though he was a little slower. Then he crawled up onto the bed and bent Lane's legs back. They were covered in soft, blond hairs. "Try and relax," he said, pressing a kiss to the arch of Lane's foot. "Tell me if there's something wrong, and I'll stop. Okay?"

"Okay."

Parker kissed Lane's other foot before sliding down to the mattress, ready to use his lips and tongue like the dog he was. If for some reason, all his reassurances failed, maybe Parker could chase Lane's fear away with pleasure.

* * *

Lane had had sex with a moderate number of guys. Probably, if he sat down and really thought about it, he could name them all. But there were the men before Adrian, there was Adrian, and then there was this.

Parker played with him for what felt like hours. He did nick him with his claws once or twice, but Lane barely noticed. The little pricks of pain in the backs of his thighs were nothing compared to the wet heat circling his hole, the blunt pressure of fingers working him open, the hot swipes over his balls and up his cock. Seeing fangs that close to his most sensitive places were scary at first. But Parker was careful to only use his tongue, and after a few minutes of attention, Lane was putty on the bed.

Was Parker ever going to fuck him? Did Lane care? He only wondered if he would get to come sometime soon. Each time Parker pushed him to the edge, he pulled him back again.

"Parker." Forming the word was more difficult than he expected. It was the first time he'd spoken since the pleasure had begun.

Parker froze and looked up at him. His eyes were embers; his face was blotchy with blood just under the skin. "Something wrong?"

"I'm gonna sweat. Don't wanna...freak you out. Stain your sheets..."

Parker crawled up Lane's body and nestled between his open legs. "Don't worry about it. Do you think you can take my cock?"

Lane's body remembered the last cock it had taken. Lukewarm, blood-tipped. He had been just as relaxed then, but from blood loss, not...trust? "Yeah."

Parker lined himself up. He was sweaty like humans got sweaty, and his body was perfect. Not muscular like he spent all his time in the gym, but fit like it was effortless. Maybe for wolves, it was. Slowly, he pushed his cock into Lane. From the first bit of pressure, Lane was hungry for it. How had he not cared about feeling this before?

"Okay?" asked Parker.

"More."

Parker laughed breathlessly. "I'm giving you all of it. Trying to be gentle."

Lane almost told him not to be, but this was kind of nice. And then he felt the thicker pressure of Parker's knot. "Holy shit," he whispered. Parker was already so deep, how...?

"You want it?"

"Uh..."

"You don't have to." Parker pulled out a little and thrust back in, sending a shock of pleasure through Lane's body. He tipped his head back and moaned.

"Just do it. I heal."

"I'm not gonna tear you, babe." He thrust in a slow rhythm, each time stopping where the knot started. Lane got a little lost. The universe encompassed only these things: Parker, himself, the bedsheets against his back, the girth stretching him. Parker's heartbeat. His.

When the knot slipped in, it was like a prick from one of Parker's claws. It hurt, but only for a second. Then Lane was crying out involuntarily as pleasure wracked him. His heart was a sledgehammer against the stone of his ribcage. Blood coated his skin, giving it a glossy sheen, and that same blood spurted from the tip of his cock as he came.

Parker pressed their foreheads together. With each of his heavy breaths, he seemed to growl a little. Inside Lane, the knot contracted, and fluid filled him.

Parker was saying something. He wasn't just growling. Lane could barely hear him over the sound of both their hearts, but then he caught it. "Mine," Parker was chanting. "Mine, mine, mine, mine..."

Blood pooled in Lane's eyes and dripped from their outer corners. Parker had made love to him, and he hadn't panicked. Instead, he had enjoyed it from beginning to end.

* * *

Parker had never felt like this with Carly. Granted, he'd never given her his knot, but that wasn't supposed to be necessary for this type of feeling. They could still have lain like this, face-to-face, blinking slowly at each other, tied or not. Lane's whole body was sticky and red. But his eyes were a calm blue, full of nothing but contentment. He was boneless. Parker drew lines in the drying blood.

"How long's it stay big like this?"

"Few more minutes." Something like fear flashed through Lane's gaze. "It's okay," said Parker. "Not much longer."

"Will you get up when it goes down?"

"Hmm?"

"Will you get up?"

Realization dawned in Parker's sex-addled brain. Maybe... Maybe Lane was scared of Parker leaving, not of being stuck together. "Not if you don't want me to. We can stay here as long as you like." Parker had noticed a while ago that Lane had blood in his eyes. Tears? He wanted to ask, but making Lane self-conscious could turn this moment sour. He'd do anything to keep that from happening.

"Maybe we can take a shower," said Lane. "My sweat's going to dry and make me itch."

"Whatever you want."

"Can I tell you something?"

Parker raked his now clawless fingers through Lane's blood-tinted, blond strands. "Anything."

"My last boyfriend was a vampire."

Parker snatched his hand away to avoid scratching Lane's scalp with his reemerging claws. "Please don't make me jealous right now."

Lane froze and shifted like he was trying to pull them apart. Parker wrapped his arm around him. "Don't. You'll hurt us both."

"Parker—"

Parker made shushing noises against Lane's ear. "I'm sorry. I'm not going to hurt you. I promise."

"Y-You said 'anything.'"

"I thought..." *Fuck.* "I thought you were going to say something romantic."

Lane laughed, but it was shaky, breathy. "What if I was?"

Parker pulled back to look in his eyes, but Lane's gaze went right to his fangs. He hadn't seemed to notice them during sex, but then again, he wasn't as distracted now. It was unclear if Lane would ever see him as more than a wolf. If he could ever handle being bitten, handle a rut. Parker's rut was as little as a month away, and he'd have to go through it alone again.

"What's wrong?" asked Lane.

"You're scared of me again."

Lane pulled his arms to his chest. "I'm not."

"This vampire ex. He hurt you with his fangs, right?"

Lane smiled, but it wasn't really a smile; it was full of pain. "Yes." His pretty blue gaze moved from Parker's eyes to his fangs, eyes to fangs. "We had a fight earlier in the night. I'd thought it was over, that we were making up, but..." Lane shrugged. "He drained me. It was at a party, but we were in his room. Too many heartbeats for anyone to notice mine disappearing, I guess. I used to love fangs."

The story made Parker feel hollow. "Is he dead?"

"Yes. The other vampires turned on him." Lane was shaking.

Parker shifted his hips, testing the size of his knot, but Lane gripped him, pulling him back close. Parker grunted.

"You won't hurt me," Lane whispered, moving his hands to Parker's head and bringing their faces together. His heart beat wetly. "You won't hurt me; I know it."

Parker thought of the claiming bite, how he'd love to sink his fangs into Lane's throat and create a mating Bond. It wouldn't work on Lane. Only Parker's wolf could feel it. And Parker would suffer because Lane would stop trusting him if he bit him before he was ready.

Would he ever be ready, though?

"Never," said Parker, and kissed him closemouthed.

CHAPTER SIX

"You smell like shifter."

Lane had been hoping to steal into the den, pick up a few things, and leave again—no drama. But Sam was standing in the foyer like he'd been waiting for Lane, and wherever Sam went, drama followed.

Erica must have let him know about Lane's whereabouts.

"That makes sense," said Lane. "I'm seeing a werewolf."

"He must be pretty hot."

Lane clenched his jaw and rolled his eyes at the same time. It was a losing game talking to Sam about anything personal. He and Lane had never been close. Ever since Lane was turned, Sam had been nearby, eying him as if he were an enemy. Now they were like coworkers, exchanging meaningless pleasantries whenever they ran into each other. Sam was just trying to make it seem like he cared about Lane, because that was what Theo wanted.

Since Theo had been gone, Lane had seen Sam less and less. He was always in his room with a human. If Sam was still showing off at den parties with his bed partners, Lane didn't know about it. He'd been missing the get-togethers to see Parker.

As Lane walked up the stairs to his room, Sam trailed him. When Lane tried to close the door on him, Sam stopped it with a deft hand.

"Is this any way to treat your elder, Lane?"

Lane was lucky it took more than a scolding to make a vampire blush. "What do you want?"

"I want to talk about what you've been doing. Running around with shifters, shirking your den—"

"That's ridiculous."

"Don't interrupt me."

Two scoldings were enough to make Lane's chest feel tight. He went farther into the room, but only because there was no place else to run. What was Sam's problem? Erica and Theo had been keeping the leash snug around Lane, and he'd made every compromise they'd insisted on.

Sam walked into the room and closed and locked the door. Lane's heart came to life. Where was Erica? Was she here? Would she hear if he called for her?

"Scared of me? Oh, please."

"I'm not scared."

"I just want to talk to you. I've heard Theo come into your room and lock the door plenty of times."

"He's my Maker."

"Does he fuck you?"

Lane laughed involuntarily. The notion, no matter how many times he'd imagined it himself, was ludicrous. "You would have heard…"

"Theo knows how to be quiet." Sam was walking closer.

Lane turned his back on Sam and wrapped his arms around himself. "The answer is no. He wouldn't dream of it, I'm pretty sure."

From behind, Sam rested one of his smooth hands on the expanse of skin between Lane's neck and shoulder, just above his T-shirt. Lane's body grew warmer. He didn't know if it was due to panic or because if he couldn't have Theo, Sam was the next best thing. Controlled and wild at the same time.

But where Sam treated Lane like an obligation, Parker treated him like a precious thing. There really wasn't any comparison.

"Maybe I hang out with shifters because they're nicer to me than you are."

Sam snatched his hand away. "Fuck you, Lane. You should be groveling after what we did for you."

Lane rounded on Sam. "*Theo* saved me. Not you. And I grovel enough."

"It was a den decision. And you know, Theo won't let this shifter shit go on for much longer. Erica coddles you, but Theo—"

"Isn't here."

Lane's time with Parker was like a salve on the hole in Lane's stomach. But Sam was opening it wide again, making it smart. Theo made phone calls when Lane acted out, but when Lane really needed him, he didn't answer. He would have cut out his heart for a hug, for Theo's forehead against his and words about how proud Theo was. But he wasn't proud. Lane was ruining any chances of that. Good.

Sam huffed and pushed his bangs back from his forehead. "He'll be back. And when he is, you'll regret rebelling like this. You're being immature and naive. Just like you were with Adrian."

Bringing up Theo when Lane missed him was mean. Bringing up Adrian... Lane's stomach turned over. "You're an ass. I'm going back to Parker's." He went to the closet to get his duffel and started filling it with clothes. Fuck Sam. He hadn't done anything for Lane. He'd only made his life worse.

"You know what I don't get?" asked Sam. "Theo lets you see this knot-dicked asshole 'Parker,' but I wasn't good enough."

Lane had shoved six shirts into his bag before he caught up with the words. "What?" He met Sam's eyes, which were hard as crystal.

"I wanted you. You're..." Sam laughed. He put his hands in his pockets and paced to the edge of the room. "You're just my type. I could be yours, too, I think. But Theo said it would confuse you to be pursued by a denmate, even now that you're older."

Sam was usually blunt, but the things he was spouting now... "You have a different human every night."

Sam looked back over his shoulder. "So?"

"You can't like me."

"Or I like you too much."

Lane turned back to the closet, pulling down a pair of jeans and packing them away. Why hadn't either of them told him about this? Sam or Theo? Why hadn't he gotten a say? God, he was tired of this place, of the vampires and their control and their secrets. He wasn't a child.

"I'm with Parker now," he said.

"I assume that's where you're going with that bag?"

Lane didn't answer. He'd been planning to go back for another night or two, but what if he stayed longer?

"Did you get permission?"

"I got it for tonight. Ask Erica."

In a flash, Sam was standing at Lane's side, nearly touching him. He looked down into Lane's duffel and lifted one side of the zipper with his index finger. "Looks like you've got more than you need."

"Yep." Lane sped over to the dresser, taking the bag with him. He packed boxers and socks.

"This isn't just about me and my feelings, you know. He could hurt you."

Once again, Lane stayed silent. He went to the bathroom and got his toothbrush. He packed up the charger for his phone. Then he zipped up the duffel and swung the strap onto his shoulder.

"If you've really had some crush on me this whole time, you've done a shitty job of showing it."

"Den leader's orders," said Sam.

"Right. Well if you talk to Theo, since he rarely talks to me, would you tell him to go fuck himself?"

Lane was boiling, but all Sam did was look at the ceiling and shake his head. "I don't think that would be wise."

So what if it wasn't? Lane was tired of being scared. He wanted to be like he'd been as a human, unafraid to jump without looking.

At least this time, he had a safety net. Parker had said he'd take him in. He'd practically ordered it.

Stalking past Sam, Lane unlocked the door and left.

* * *

Parker was happy to have Lane at the house, and Heather had assured them both that she didn't mind if he stayed for a while. But something had clearly changed for Lane in the hour or so he'd been at his den. Something he was reluctant to talk about even days later.

Instead, all he seemed to want to do was have sex.

Parker didn't entirely mind. He tried to use it as an opportunity to understand Lane better, at least when his wolf wasn't taking over his brain. Lane didn't tire like another shifter would have. He didn't need a night's sleep between knottings, or even the few minutes recovery time that Parker had to take with a smoke break.

Each time Parker slid inside of him, Lane got more adventurous with Parker's claws and fangs. While riding him, Lane would put Parker's paw on his pec and ask him to use his claws on his nipples. When underneath him, Lane would put a hand on Parker's face and touch his lips whenever he closed them.

"I need to see them. Please."

Maybe Lane was trying to desensitize himself. Parker wanted to help him get to wherever he needed to be, but with each degree of intimacy, his urge to claim Lane grew stronger. Humans judged their relationships by length of time. Wolves judged by the strength of the connection and the willingness to command or submit. Lane wasn't ready to submit fully yet. But each time he threw his head back in ecstasy, Parker zeroed in on the sensitive flesh of his throat. And each time, to stave off the yearning to bite him there, he offered Lane a wrist.

Over a week passed before Parker finally got Lane to talk to him.

"What happened? You know I can tell something's wrong."

Lane focused sated, sex-drunk eyes on Parker and shrugged. He was sitting on top again, resting his hands on Parker's chest while he waited for the knot to go down.

"If you want to be with me, you have to talk to me. I'm sick of you dodging my questions." Just last night, Lane had pretended to sleep to avoid this conversation.

Now, he sighed petulantly. "You don't like it when I make you jealous."

So Lane clamming up was *his* fault. Parker put his paws on top of Lane's hands and spoke as evenly as he could. "Did someone touch you?" It helped a little that he was tired. Lane had more stamina than he did for all this fucking.

"No. I promise." Lane slipped a hand out from under Parker's paw and drew the tip of his finger from Parker's forehead down the bridge of his nose. "No one but you."

Something in Parker's chest unlocked. "Did someone hurt you? Threaten to hurt you? Do I need to protect you?"

"No. I'm safe."

Parker exhaled. "Okay. Tell me what happened."

Lane brushed his fingers over Parker's scalp, which made Parker's eyelids heavy. "My denmate Sam told me he has a crush on me."

Parker snapped his eyes fully open. "Seriously? Do you like him back?"

"No." Lane chuckled. "But apparently he's had it bad for me for like, years or something. Theo knew, and he told Sam he wasn't allowed to do anything about it. All this without including me. And Sam kept saying you're going to hurt me, and that pissed me off, too, so I left. I'm tired of their crap."

Maybe this was the time Parker should mention it. His urge to bite and claim, to do the very thing to Lane he'd promised he wouldn't.

"What's wrong?" asked Lane. Sometimes Parker's emotions sprouted onto his face like weeds; obviously, this was one of those times.

"I need to talk to you about something."

Parker felt Lane's frown in his gut.

"What?"

"Something about being a wolf. It's a problem, but we'll figure it out. Okay?"

"Okay..."

Parker had been taught that as an Alpha, one didn't have to be eloquent. One barked orders, and that was that. But then, his father had expected him to mate with a so-called "strong omega," not a vampire with fanged monsters in his past. He watched Lane's face closely as he'd probably fail to say this the right way. "The more time we spend together, the more I want to bite you."

Lane swallowed. "Parker..."

"Not in a violent way. I mean... It's loving. It's because I want you like that. Mine. Bonded." He got heady just thinking about it; if he didn't relax, his knot would refill. But maybe Lane wouldn't mind. "I'm not going to do it." He leaned his head back, away from the vulnerable body on top of him. "I feel sleazy thinking like that when you're so scared of them."

"It's getting better, though."

The last thing Parker wanted to do was pressure him. Alphas didn't push their omegas further than they could go. But... "I'm not going to do it. I'm just telling you about it."

"But you *want* to do it. And what about the next full moon? Heather said it was brutal."

Parker didn't want to discuss that or his rut, which was coming up a lot sooner than he was ready for. Yesterday had marked the first day of December, and his rut could take hold of him any time between now and the beginning of March. And even if it happened later, there was still the full moon on December thirteenth.

Unfortunately, communicating was important even when it made things harder. "You can go somewhere else during those times. I'll pay for a hotel room."

"No." Lane crossed his arms, a closed-off gesture in contrast to the tie between their legs. "I'm not letting you hook up with someone who's not me."

"I wouldn't do that. I'll go through it alone."

"Does that hurt you? Is it harder?"

"I'll live." He pulled his brows together as Lane pouted. It seemed he might cry, and Parker couldn't stand that. He sat up, bringing them closer, and brushed their noses together. "I wasn't trying to upset you, baby."

"Okay."

"It's not necessary for me to bite you." Wasn't it? Parker shoved the notion aside. "You can bite my neck instead. I give you permission."

Lane kissed Parker. "Now?"

"Yes. It helps calm me down anyway." The words felt forbidden in his mouth. Only omegas felt that way about being bitten. But it was true; feeling Lane's teeth in his skin got rid of the urge to claim at least for a little while.

Lane dipped his head, nuzzling Parker's neck. "I like it when you call me 'baby,'" he whispered. "Nobody's ever called me that."

Parker grinned. "Bite me, baby." He wasn't afraid of teeth, but he was afraid of what Lane might do to him. Make him feel bonded and then run. Pathetic. Alphas took what they wanted. Someday, Parker would have to find a way to make Lane surrender.

Lane bit down, and not for the first time, Parker was the one who surrendered.

* * *

Both Parker and Heather were at work. It was the first time Lane had been left to his own devices since he'd started staying at

Heather's, a freedom he'd never experienced at the den, considering there was always at least one elder present in the mansion. Probably, he should have taken the opportunity to masturbate or something. But he'd been having so much sex with Parker he wasn't hungry in that regard.

It was while lying on his back in bed that the idea struck him. It was a bad idea, one he knew Parker would never approve of. But on the other hand, it had the potential to solve the one problem putting distance between them: Lane's inability to take Parker's fangs. The other stuff—Lane's elders, all the annoying shit that went along with being a vampire—didn't seem to bother Parker. But Lane knew from their conversation about biting how important it was to him. Lane had to fix this. He had to fix *himself*. And he would get Sam to help him.

Tonight would be the perfect setup. He knew if he showed up at the den to talk to Sam, he'd risk Erica swarming him, even though he'd been keeping her updated with daily text messages. Sam's info was in Lane's phone, too (Theo insisted on it), but this would be the first time he'd texted him.

I need your help with something. Tonight. It's time sensitive and it has to be kept secret

Admittedly, Lane could have waited. Heather and Parker would work on the same night again. But by then, he would have lost his nerve to go through with this risky plan. And how long was Parker going to stick around waiting for Lane to give him what he needed? He'd already lost Theo; he didn't want to lose Parker, too. It would be great to stop thinking about the past all the time; he was tired of the weight on his heart. If going through with his idea made him remember just a little bit less when he was in Parker's arms, it would be worth it.

What is it?

Lane gulped as he stared at his phone. Sickness swirled in his gut as he imagined what Parker would think of his plan. If he found out, he'd be devastated. But if it worked...

Parker would never have to know.

I need you to bite me

Lane jumped when his phone buzzed immediately. Damn speedy vampire fingers.

I'm going to need a bit more information, Lane.

Lane exhaled testily. Really? Sam was all into him but needed to be persuaded to get close? Lane paced on the back porch. He still had five hours until Parker's shift was over, but he needed to be home well before Parker got back. He'd need to make sure he was free of any blood and scents that would signify he'd been with Sam.

I need help getting over my fear of being bitten. I trust you. Please

He trusted him not to hurt him, anyway. He didn't trust him not to scheme and lie. But Lane couldn't see a better option. Yes, he could do this with Parker. But Parker wanted it so bad. What if Lane couldn't do it? What if he told Parker he could try and got his hopes up for nothing? He'd panic, and Parker would dump him, and all the soft, loving moments he'd had in his arms would be nothing more than memories. It would be better to find out. At worst, he could end things first, so at least he'd only be tearing out his own heart. It wouldn't be like when Theo had left without him. And if it took more than one night with Sam to prepare himself for Parker's fangs, then that was fine.

Fine. Meet me at the den.

Lane exhaled on a grin. *Thank you so much. But Erica can't see me... She can't know*

Lane paced the length of the back porch several times before Sam responded. *I've enchanted one of her humans to distract her. She won't see you get here.*

Making sure all the buttons of his winter coat were secured, Lane set off into the suburban depths on foot.

CHAPTER SEVEN

With Heather at her other gig at Brewhaha, Parker was left with a bitchy bird shifter as his night manager. Apparently he couldn't pour drinks fast enough, or he'd made them too strong on the rare occasion someone ordered a mixed drink. And he'd gotten a few orders wrong what with her breathing down his neck and making him nervous. He also hadn't gotten much in the way of tips. So when he pulled in to the driveway around three in the morning, he wasn't in the best of moods.

Maybe a shower and a nice long fuck session with Lane would make him feel better. He had tomorrow off. He could sleep in with his nocturnal vampire, hold his skinny limbs close, and rest with him safe at his side.

Parker locked the door behind him and dropped his keys on the coffee table. The house was eerily quiet. He kept his ears peeled as he strode farther into the house, listening for heartbeats and movements. But there were none. Both bedrooms were empty, the kitchen and bathrooms dark. Heather must have gone to Rina's after work, but Lane?

Fear and anger poured into him in equal measure. He whipped out his phone. *Where the fuck are you?* But when he read the text back, he winced. He couldn't be the typical overbearing Alpha if he wanted to keep Lane. He'd frighten him. It was enough that he couldn't stop staring at his neck and that he'd told Lane just why he was doing it. *Sorry. I'm just worried.*

No answer. Parker waited twenty more minutes before he let himself freak out.

Maybe Lane had stopped by the den to pick up more of his stuff. No way could the few pieces of clothing he'd brought in that duffel be all he owned. Parker looked around to make sure the duffel was still there, and it was. So he hadn't decided to move out without telling him, at least.

Why hadn't he told him where he was going, though? Or texted him to let him know he'd be gone so late? Maybe ten minutes past three in the morning wasn't late for a vampire, but Parker deserved to know where his mate was.

Mate. He growled at himself for even thinking the word. They weren't mates yet, and if Parker didn't get a handle on his wolf, they never would be.

He called Lane.

"This is Lane's phone." The voice was male, and just that had Parker on the cusp of a jealous rage. Because if whoever had Lane's phone wasn't someone to be jealous of, he was someone to protect Lane from, which was arguably worse.

"Where is he?"

"The den. Had a bit of trouble controlling his hunger, but don't worry, we'll have him back to you soon enough." If Parker wasn't mistaken, the man sounded put-upon, as if Parker didn't deserve the half-assed update. And if Lane really was at the den, who could this man be but Sam? The very vampire who had confessed to having feelings for Lane? *His* Lane.

"Let me talk to him."

"He's asleep. I'll tell him you called."

Parker was about to tell him he'd better put him on the phone right goddamn now when Sam hung up. Parker growled long and low. His hands sprouted claws and then turned to wolf paws, sending his phone dropping onto the carpet. His whole body cracked and bent as it transformed.

He hadn't shifted involuntarily since he was a pup, but he'd also never cared this much about anyone aside from his little sister, who wasn't nearly as frustrating as Lane. Luckily, he kept his wits about him, but only enough to shove his nose in Lane's duffel and memorize the scent of his blood. Then he set off toward wherever that scent would take him—hopefully, to Lane's den.

* * *

Lane's bed at the den was of the highest quality. The memory foam mattress cradled his limbs as if it had been manufactured for his body alone, and the sheets were as soft as flower petals. When he awakened, it was with a smile. Then reality hit him like a stinging slap to the face.

He needed to check his phone. It wasn't on the nightstand or in the pocket of his jeans. At least he was still *wearing* his jeans. He was shirtless, and there was dried blood caked at his throat and cheeks. His groin itched from the dried blood there, too, but he ignored it.

The clock on the wall said 3:20 a.m. *Shit.* Parker would be home by now, and there was no way he wouldn't notice Lane missing. Lane looked around for his shirt but couldn't find it, so he got a new one from his dresser and put it on.

Fuck. Nothing had gone according to plan tonight, and now he'd have to explain himself. He'd have to tell Parker that instead of panicking when Sam had bitten him, he'd gotten turned on. So turned on that his dick had leaked. Only then had Lane panicked, losing his shit so completely that Sam had had to get Erica to help subdue him. Which meant Erica knew about Sam being alone with him and doing something that looked very much like breaking Theo's rule. What if Erica told Theo about it? Would Sam get in trouble? Would Lane? Would he be able to keep staying with Parker? Would Parker even want him there?

Lane left his bedroom and sped down the stairs. He found Sam and Erica alone in the great room. They must have made all the humans leave.

"Where's my phone?" he asked Sam.

"Lane..." Erica stood up.

"Right here." Sam pulled the cell out of his pocket and handed it to him, but when Lane turned to leave, Sam caught him from behind around the middle. "Where are you going? We need to talk about this."

Lane struggled in Sam's hold. "I'm going home."

"You *are* home," said Erica, frowning.

He didn't want to upset her, but he *had* to go. He had to talk to Parker, try to do damage control. He hadn't freaked out. He'd *liked* the bite. Which meant he was probably okay to take Parker's fangs. He could let Parker claim him, could fix the pain in Parker's eyes when he couldn't seem to stop staring at his throat. Lane knew hunger when he saw it. Parker always sated his, and now Lane could return the favor.

If only Sam would let him go.

He continued to fight the hold. Erica came to stand in front of him and reached out to lift each of his eyebrows, checking his eyes for hunger-induced dilation. "He won't attack anyone. You can let him go."

Sam didn't. "His boyfriend's a wolf, Erica. They're possessive. He'll smell me on him and hurt him."

"Do you want me to tell Theo what you did?" At the sound of her voice, trembling but furious, Lane froze. Thank God her gaze was focused on Sam and not him. It was as if at any moment, her hair would turn to snakes, and Sam, who was already so unyielding around him, would turn to stone. "You took advantage of him."

"If anyone took advantage of anyone, it was Lane."

A flash of movement, a slice, a whimper. Sam let go of Lane so suddenly that he fell to the floor. When Lane looked up, he saw three bleeding scratches on Sam's cheek.

"He is our youngest member," said Erica. "You are his elder. Act like it." She extended her hand, bloody skin under her nails, and helped Lane to his feet. "You may go. I expect to hear from you in thirty minutes with an update."

Lane didn't set off immediately, but only because he paused to give Erica a quick kiss on her pale cheek. She was a Gorgon, but she loved him. Lane knew that deep in his heart. "He won't hurt me, Erica. He loves me." Parker had never said it, but somehow Lane knew it, too.

Erica nodded, and Lane fled the great room, heading out into the night at full speed. He barely got past the gate before he rammed into something solid.

His back hit dewy grass. Two wet paws held him down at his shoulders, seeping moisture through the thin layer of his cotton T-shirt. A mouth with two rows of sharp, shining teeth opened above him, letting out a rumbling growl that seemed to shake the very earth under him.

Oh, God. Parker. Lane was too shocked to speak.

Slowly, wolf fur receded into human skin, but the fangs and orange eyes remained. A naked, partially shifted Parker kept Lane pinned to the grass. "You've been bleeding," he said.

Lane was trembling, but he forced out words. "I'm okay."

Parker licked Lane's face where his tears had dried. He licked his throat and sniffed. "What happened? Sam said you were hungry. I don't understand."

Technically, it was true. Lane's panic, as it often did with vampires, had morphed into hunger. The only thing that had been able to calm him was blood. Erica had tried to give him a reasonable amount, but he'd protested until she'd let him drink himself to sleep. He hadn't been coherent enough to think about the consequences of that.

"Parker, I'm okay now. Let's just go home."

"Tell me what happened!"

Lane flinched at the shout. Parker didn't apologize for scaring him like he usually did. Would Parker hurt him if he told him the truth? He was clearly angry now, but he hadn't actually threatened him. Where he held him down, his claws hadn't broken skin.

"You're going to be mad," Lane said, stalling. "You'll hate me."

Parker's glowing gaze bored into Lane's. "Tell me what you did with him. Tell me!"

Seeing no other option, Lane took a breath and let the truth spill. "I had to know if I could handle it before I did it with you, so I had Sam bite me. Please, Parker. Please don't hurt me. I did it to make sure we had a chance."

* * *

It was as if Lane had speared him with a blade. The pain was a solid thing, lancing him in the chest and gut and threatening to send him into another involuntary shift. Parker managed to hold his wolf back, but he couldn't touch Lane any longer or he'd lose control. He stood, naked as he was, his clawed feet digging into the soil.

"I'm not going to hurt you," he growled. *Even if you did the claiming bite with someone else.* It couldn't be the same for vampires; Lane probably didn't see it as claiming. But to Parker, it was a betrayal. Lane had *known* how important it was to him, and yet he'd gone to Sam? The very vampire who harbored feelings for him?

Parker's wolf screamed to go hunt. Maybe he'd sink his teeth into some animals, run around close to where humans lived until he got shot.

"Are you going to say something?" Lane remained on the ground, propped up on his hands.

"Like what?"

"I don't know. I didn't do it to make you jealous. I just wanted to see if I could do it. Parker, you can bite me. I can handle it. Everything's going to be okay with us."

Parker's wolf was a torrent of pain and secondary anger, but his human side balked at Lane's logic. "Were we not okay before?"

Lane's face fell. "Of course we were. I just... You wanted to bite me. I wanted to make it happen. That's all." He leaned his head back, baring his throat. "You can do it now. Go ahead."

It made him queasy—the thought of putting his fangs where someone else's had just been. How could Lane think he would want that? How could he have explored the possibility of claiming with someone other than him? Parker would have rather not bitten him at all.

"I can't. I don't want to."

"Parker." Lane sat up. There was blood coming out of his eyes. "Let's just go home. I didn't mean to stay here so late. Please."

Home. With Lane? In his bed? He imagined smelling his subtle iron scent, imagined holding him in sleep, keeping him warm even after his heart went quiet. The images made him ache, but they didn't hold the same appeal now that Lane had betrayed him like this. Even though Lane was here, ready to give Parker what he wanted, his wolf couldn't help but feel like another wolf had fought him for Lane and won. Sam had won.

The blade sliced through Parker all over again. Lane had been the first person he'd truly wanted to mate with, but now his wolf was turnings its back. Parker couldn't do anything but follow.

"Go back to your den," he said. The pain choked him, as if he were bleeding internally. "Heather can bring your stuff over sometime later. I don't want to see you right now."

"What?" Lane got to his feet.

Parker crouched, ready to shift back into wolf form so he could run home. "You heard me. It's done. We're done. Go back to your den."

Lane's face was streaked with blood now. He dropped to his knees next to Parker and tried to pull him close, but Parker shifted and growled.

"No," said Lane. "You can't mean that. I didn't have sex with him! I just wanted to be good enough for you. You're overreacting." He choked out a sob. "*God.*"

Parker lunged forward, teeth bared. Even though he didn't want to give Lane the mating bite, he still wanted to see him submit and surrender to the stronger beast.

Lane was shaking all over, but he didn't back down. He didn't shut up. "I'm not scared of you. I want to be with you. I'm yours, Parker. Sam is nothing. He's nothing!"

Parker's wolf protested the words. Lane wasn't his. They hadn't bonded. He shoved him back with his paws and growled in his face until Lane stopped pleading, until he had his arms up and could only whimper and quiver.

He was just a baby. A baby vampire. No bark, no bite.

Satisfied, Parker set off away from the opulence of Bloomfield Hills toward the cracked-cement reality of Ferndale. His human side tried to get a word in: *Maybe after I've calmed down. Maybe—*

But Parker's wolf howled. No maybes.

CHAPTER EIGHT

Lane had cried a few civilized tears when Theo left for his summit in Switzerland. Vampires were allowed that. But they weren't allowed to stay in their rooms for days on end, looking at moon charts and fretting while their faces turned into murder scenes.

He cried so much that he had to keep a blood bag in the mini fridge near the foot of his bed to replenish the lost blood. Erica and Sam wouldn't leave him alone. Each of them visited him at least once per night trying to get him to come down to the great room and have a human, to socialize.

He couldn't do that. He didn't want to move an inch—unless it would bring him closer to Parker. And he knew for a fact that Parker was *not* in the great room; he wouldn't even answer Lane's texts.

A few nights after Parker had broken things off, Heather came by with Lane's duffel bag. Lane left his room long enough to meet her outside, since she still wasn't allowed inside the den. Her features were hard, her gaze fiery. Lane knew before she spoke that she'd taken Parker's side.

She dropped his duffel on the grass by the wrought iron gate set in the fence that surrounded the property.

"Thanks," he said.

"How are you doing?"

An alien smile stretched Lane's lips. "Do you care?"

"Of course I do!" Heather thumped the outside of Lane's arm with the back of her hand. "How can you say that? I care about both of you. And I'm mad at both of you."

"Tell him to text me back."

"Did you apologize to him?"

Lane had to laugh at that. He looked down at the sneakers he hadn't bothered to tie. "I literally begged him. On my knees. It was pretty undignified." He laughed again, because if he didn't laugh, he was going to come apart right here. "He doesn't want me."

"That's not true. He wants you very much; he's just being stubborn. And he's never wanted to mate with somebody so bad before. That's what he said."

Lane tried to tune the words out. None of that helped him. "He doesn't want to *be* with me. Is that better?"

Heather crossed her arms, the faux leather of her jacket squeaking. "You want my advice?"

"Why not?"

"His rut's coming up. You know, mating season?"

Lane knew what it meant in theory, anyway. "Yeah, yeah."

"Could be in a few days or a few months. But if you really want to be with him, you should make yourself available for it. It would mean a lot to him."

Lane had offered himself up several times over the last few nights, only to be greeted by silence. But he hadn't tried this tactic. Would he be willing to put himself at the mercy of Parker's wolf? Let him bite and claw and fuck for... Well he didn't know how long it would last. But it didn't matter. Despite the fear that clogged his throat, the answer to all that was yes.

It wasn't as if *Parker* would say yes.

"Okay," said Lane.

Heather looked off into the distance.

"How are things with Rina?" Lane asked.

"Great. We worked things out. Actually, we're thinking about moving in together."

We worked things out. Like it was so easy. But nothing about relationships was easy. Not even if evolution forced a Bond on you.

He cleared his throat. "That's awesome." Where would Parker go if she moved out? Could he afford the place on his own? Not that that was Heather's responsibility, and it definitely wasn't Lane's.

"The main thing with me and Rina is that we don't cheat on each other," said Heather.

It took Lane a moment to parse the accusation. "What? I didn't—"

"That's the way he sees it. He's a typical possessive Alpha. That's how they are."

Defensive anger beat beneath Lane's skin. Was she trying to help him or make him want to die? "He didn't give me a chance to explain. He doesn't know anything."

"I know dating a shifter is difficult. It's not for everybody. But if you're serious about him, do what I said about the rut. *If* you can do it. I'm mad at him too because he pushed you too hard. If he hadn't, you might not have gone to Sam, so I don't want to do that to you, too. I just think... Well, you seemed so happy with him."

The words were like nails in Lane's chest, scratching him. They taunted him with what he no longer had, and brought embarrassing tears to his eyes. He wiped them away as soon as they fell. "Parker didn't push me. Okay?" Well, maybe he had, but Lane hadn't minded. It had been refreshing compared to how Theo seemed to tiptoe around him, keeping everything secret and restrained. "I can handle the rut. If he needs to bite and claw me to talk to me, fine." Anything to make the sadness stop. Missing Parker and Theo at the same time was too much.

"Can I give you a hug?" asked Heather.

"No." He'd only get blood on her jacket. "You know us vamps. Don't show affection."

"Right." She gave him a sad smile. "I need to go."

Lane scratched at the back of his neck. "I'm really happy for you and Rina. Seriously."

"Thank you."

Lane watched as Heather got back into her beat-up car and headed down the little road that would take her back to Woodward Ave. Then he went back inside and up to his room.

* * *

"You don't want to pay six bucks for a shot? Don't order top shelf." It was a vaguely antagonistic statement that shouldn't have led to an all-out brawl between Parker and a skinny alligator who turned out to be a lot stronger than he looked. But the full moon was fast approaching, and Parker was hardly handling it well. In just a few days, Meta would put a hold on booze sales and close its doors to anyone but shifters who needed shelter. Parker wouldn't need such shelter this time, but with the way Heather kept talking about moving in with Rina, he might in January.

All that on top of losing Lane...

He couldn't blame his boss for telling him all his shifts were canceled until after the December full moon. Now he would be broke as well as depressed. Perfect.

If only Lane would stop texting him.

Can we talk? Please

I'm sorry

He'd sent those the night of their breakup, followed by a few calls that Parker let go straight to voicemail. Parker listened to the messages, during which Lane was obviously crying, but nowhere in them did Lane give a satisfying explanation. What he'd said that night at his den—*"I wanted to see if I could"*—wasn't enough. Parker could have helped him see. The fact that Lane hadn't trusted Parker said everything he needed to know about their failed relationship. If it had even counted as a relationship. How long had they been together anyway? A month?

Heather disagreed; she thought they'd been perfect together. And she'd been anything but quiet about their breakup. *"You dumped him? You've got to cut him some slack! His last boyfriend killed him, Parker."*

As if he didn't know that. But it didn't cancel out the cut in his chest. Maybe he wasn't up to the task of building a relationship around Lane's issues. He certainly hadn't been up to it with Carly. Yes, he'd been struggling with his sexuality and being accepted in his pack. But it wasn't about gender. It hadn't been mandatory for him to tell her about his bisexuality.

Unfortunately, Parker wasn't good at lying. Lies tormented him; for him, they could ruin a relationship. Maybe with Lane, he'd demanded too much too soon, or maybe he was more sensitive than any Alpha should be. But that was just who he was.

Lane needed someone of his own kind who wasn't scared to be with him. As much as it hurt Parker to think it, someone like Sam. Because Parker *was* scared. He wouldn't have admitted it out loud to anyone, but if it hurt this bad to lose Lane four weeks in, how would he feel if he lost him later or after they'd bonded? It wasn't worth it. He needed a wolf. A submissive omega whose hole would get wet at the mere thought of Parker's claiming bite. Not someone who'd tense up and cover his eyes, or worry secretly and then betray him in some misguided attempt to make things work.

Too bad Parker still wanted to sink his teeth into Lane's smooth, undead throat.

On the night Parker got suspended from work, Lane texted him again.

When is your rut?

This was Heather's doing, Parker was sure. A few days before, she'd gone to Lane's den to bring him his things, and it was highly possible she'd put ideas about Parker's rut in Lane's head. As Parker read the text, the aches Lane had caused him smarted under the throbbing bites and scratches courtesy of that alligator. He still hadn't decided what to answer when Lane followed it up.

I know you hate me. You'd probably prefer to hook up with a shifter but I'm here for you. Ok?

Jesus. More assumptions! Parker wanted to claw every stupid thought from Lane's head. *Hate you? Hardly. And I won't be hooking up with anyone. You think I want to hook up with some stranger right now?*

I don't know

Well I don't.

Ok. Let me know if you change your mind

That was it. No begging, no apologies, nothing that made Parker want to forgive him. He didn't know what Lane needed to say, but he knew he hadn't heard it yet.

It's more than a one-night commitment.

How many nights?

5–7 days and nights. There'd be breaks in between, but we'd be tied a lot as well. He was talking about it like it was a possibility, but it wasn't, was it?

Could I drink from you?

A little, but I'd need my energy.

I'd bring blood bags. I can take it

Lane was getting his hopes up. Parker could feel his excitement in how fast he answered each text.

We'll become Bonded.

There was a long pause after that one.

Please explain

My wolf will become mated to you. If we stay broken up, it'll wear off, but for a while, I won't be able to stay away from you. You'll have to block my number, ignore me completely.

What about me? Will I feel a Bond?

No. I'd suffer alone.

But you won't suffer if you take me back

The words had Parker's wolf stirring. But none of it was going to happen. Lane wasn't going to help Parker through his rut. They weren't going to get back together. He tried to make his wolf understand even as it prepared to claw its way to the surface.

Won't I? Parker knew he was being cold, but he felt cold. He'd packed the hole in his chest with ice in a desperate attempt to make the swelling go down.

No. If you take me back, I'll leave my den. I'll never talk to Sam again. I don't like it here. I didn't like it before I met you. It's Theo's house, and even when he comes back, I'll feel like shit. He always makes me feel like shit but you don't. Heather said I cheated on you but I didn't, I swear. It wasn't like that.

Parker tried to keep his heart frozen, but his wolf demanded to know if there was still hope. Was Lane free to be claimed? He forced his wolf down.

What would you call what you did if not cheating?

Checking to see if I was too broken to be with you

Remember when you were mad at Sam for keeping his feelings a secret? You did the same to me. You assumed I would turn my back on you, but I was ready to fight for you.

I'm so sorry. What will make you fight for me now?

He still didn't have an answer. And his wolf was pacing in the back of his brain, couldn't make up its damn mind. *I'll text you when my rut starts if I feel like it.*

Ok :(

* * *

Parker's bad mood lasted three more days. Then the sex dreams started. Under normal circumstances, he dreamed about sex every once in a while, but these had him waking up feverish and unable to get back to sleep unless he made himself come. The dreams were a surefire sign he was on the cusp of losing himself to the sexual need of his rut. And his wolf wanted Lane.

He told himself it was only because of Lane's offer. There was nobody else he was interested in, and Lane was the last person he'd fucked. That didn't mean it was a good idea to call him and break both their hearts. But he'd awakened Heather yelling Lane's name so many times that she'd threatened to call him herself.

"I'll lie and tell him you asked me to. You were too out of your mind to do it."

He nearly was. The images his brain conjured were sweaty, bloody, and forbidden, given their broken-up status. But Lane had practically thrown himself at Parker with those texts. He'd offered to give up everything for another chance. So Parker knew all he had to do was ask, and Lane would be there, ready and willing to relieve him. They could make those sweaty, bloody dreams come true.

Heather stood in the doorway in the early morning, her bedhead a frizzy halo around her sternly set face. "I'm dealing with my own full moon, you know. I want to spend it with Rina. So either Lane comes to watch you, or I cover you with silver and Rina comes here."

"Cover me with silver and leave. It doesn't matter." At the very least, he was planning to wear some on his wrist anyway. The silver would weaken him enough so that he wouldn't lose control and go on some wolf rampage around town.

"That's irresponsible, and you know it." She put her hands on her hips. "What's it gonna be? Am I calling him, or are you?"

It was still dark outside. Lane could run here from Bloomfield Hills in just a few minutes. "I'll call him."

Heather didn't sound very enthused when she said, "Awesome," and slammed his door shut from the outside.

Parker reached for his phone, angling his clawed thumb to carefully navigate to Lane's name in his contacts. Texting anything coherent with his claws out and his mind in the gutter would be almost impossible. He tried to shut out said gutter thoughts—Lane on his back, baring his throat, that blood sweat all over him because that was how Parker knew he was *really* aroused—as he put the phone to his ear.

"Hello?"

"Hey. Rut's starting soon." He nearly choked on the words. "Can you come?"

Lane dropped his voice to a whisper. "One second." Then there was a *whoosh* as Lane most likely ran somewhere more private. He was still whispering when he next spoke, though. "Can you give me till after sunrise?"

"Thought you couldn't be in the sun."

"I'll cover up. Don't want Erica and Sam catching me before I leave. They might try to stop me."

"All right. See you soon."

Parker ended the call and looked at the time, groaning. Sunrise was almost three hours away. He'd probably be in control of himself for another eighteen to twenty-four, but he went into his closet to get his silver handcuffs anyway. Better safe than sorry. He was going to hurt Lane during the rut; there was no avoiding that. But he could at least try to make it a gradual thing. Maybe some Alphas had fantasies of taking omegas by force, but Parker had never gotten off on that. He wanted surrender, and he wanted the one surrendering to take pleasure in it.

As soon as Lane got here, he would do his best to make him ready for what was to come.

* * *

Lane didn't slow down long enough to be scared. He put on a nice, blood-free face for his elders, pretended to go to bed, and then waited about an hour for everyone to fall asleep. They could still catch him, but Sam was a heavy sleeper, and Erica's room was all the way at the end of the hall. While he was waiting, he got everything ready: long sleeves, pants, sunglasses, gloves, hat. He looked like he was about to rob a bank or something. He filled his duffel with clean clothes, shoved all the blood bags from his mini fridge in there, too, and secured the duffel over his shoulder with the strap across his body.

He was all set to flee, but as soon as he stepped into the hallway, he caught sight of a male human. He should have paid more attention, listened for stray heartbeats.

The human had brown skin, dark hair, and wide, startled eyes. Lane pulled the door shut behind him slowly, as quietly as he could, and put a finger to his lips. Had the human been coming out of Sam's room next door? It was likely. Erica almost always took girls upstairs.

Mercifully, the human nodded. He even mimed a little "my lips are sealed" gesture before tossing an imaginary key behind him.

"Thank you," Lane mouthed. Then he tiptoed down the stairs, into the foyer, and out the door.

The fear caught up with him as he stood on Heather and Parker's back porch. He needed to get inside. He was safe with most of his skin covered, standing under the shade of the porch's awning, but his instincts still prodded him to take cover from the sun as soon as possible. His instincts also told him there was a monster in there. One who might pounce as soon as he entered. One who was going to make him lose blood. Would he have time to put the blood bags in the fridge before Parker started fucking him? Just how out of control was he going to be?

After a few minutes, one of the heartbeats from inside came closer to the door. Lane froze. But it was only Heather.

"Hey." She was dressed in leggings and a T-shirt, her hair in a ponytail. "He's still lucid, so you don't have to stand out here like a freak." Her smile took the sting out of the insult.

"Okay."

"Nice sunglasses, though." She stepped back, holding the door open for him.

Lane went inside. "I need to put these blood bags in the fridge."

"I'll do it." She held a hand out for the duffel. "I'll leave this in the hallway?"

"Sure."

She gave Lane a peck on the cheek. "Everything's going to be fine. If you get scared, submit. Show him your throat."

"Um, okay."

She smiled once more before heading into the kitchen. Lane slipped off his hat and sunglasses and left them on the kitchen table before making his way to Parker's bedroom, his waking heartbeat preceding him. If he were human, his hands would have been sweating inside his gloves.

Parker's door was closed. Lane knocked and received a gruff "Come in" in return. What greeted him inside was a sweaty Parker in nothing but boxers, the thin fabric tented with a hard-on.

Lane couldn't help but stare. "Hi."

"Hi." Around Parker's wrist was a silver cuff, its mate attached to the bedpost. Lane's cock twitched. Not that he was particularly into handcuffs, but there was something appealing about a helpless, wanting Parker. "It's okay," said Parker, smiling, but he looked pained. "I promise. C'mere."

Lane took a few tentative steps closer. "What's that for?" he said, pointing to the cuff.

"Just a precaution. We can take it off."

"Where's the key?"

Parker pointed a claw toward the edge of the room. On the floor by the baseboard, silver glinted. Lane went over, and it took a few tries to pick up the tiny key with his gloves on. "Silver hurts you, huh?"

"Yeah."

"Me, too."

"Sorry."

Lane moved to the side of the bed, his shins brushing the mattress. Parker reached across his own sweaty torso to pick lightly at the black denim over Lane's hip.

Lane's movements stuttered. "Is it really a good idea for me to unlock this?" Parker probably couldn't give an objective answer, but there was nobody else to ask.

Parker grinned, fangs extended. It wasn't a nice grin. "If you want, you can leave me like this. Sit over there"—Parker pointed to the edge of the room—"and watch me tear the bed apart to get to you when my rut starts."

Lane swallowed. "Thought it already started."

"Not yet. Which means I can get you worked up first so it's less scary. Unlock the damn cuff."

The anger in Parker's voice brought Lane back to the grass outside his den, dew soaking into his back, Parker's teeth above him. But he fought past the fear trying to freeze him up and put the key in the lock. As he slipped the silver away, Parker sat up and then pulled Lane into the *V* of his legs.

Lane let the cuffs hit the floorboards. Parker wrapped his arm around him and nosed and sniffed at his belly and chest. He snaked his hand up the back of Lane's turtleneck and tickled his spine with his claws.

Lane's cock swelled. Secretly, he wanted to feel those claws scratch, maybe break a little skin. But if he let Parker do that, he might take it too far...

Parker sat back. "Get naked."

Vines of nervousness twisted into Lane's muscles. He turned his back on Parker and pulled off his turtleneck, toed off his sneakers, and shoved down his pants. As soon as his ass was naked, Parker wrapped his arms around his body from behind, gnawing bluntly at his right ass cheek. Still so gentle. Would he bite him now or when he wasn't "lucid" anymore?

"Are you going to forgive me after this?" asked Lane in a small voice. He turned around in Parker's embrace and put his hands on his burning-hot shoulders.

Parker's eyes glowed threateningly as he wrapped careful fingers around the base of Lane's dick. "Maybe."

Lane figured he'd have to settle for that. Parker licked the tip of his cock and then stood and shoved him face-first on the bed. He then palmed Lane's cockhead until bloody precome colored the tender skin.

Lane tried to fall into it, to focus on Parker's hands and tongue on him and the pleasure in his body instead of the uncertainty in his heart. It almost worked.

CHAPTER NINE

Parker's human side was butting in, that was the problem. His wolf wanted to claim and give pleasure, but Parker was still hurting. Their dynamic was different now. Lane had touched another—he had gotten pleasure from another—and Parker no longer thought of him as his potential mate.

But his wolf didn't care about the emotional side of mating right now. It was ready to breed the best available hole, and Lane was that, even if their mating wouldn't make pups.

They'd been at it for about twenty minutes now.

"Come on." Lane was underneath Parker, legs wrapped around him, arching and damn near begging for Parker's knot. Parker was inside him. With just a little push, his knot would be in him, too, but he couldn't do it. The rut hadn't fully overtaken him, which meant the power was not yet with his wolf. "Parker," Lane whined, "I can take it. Why are you going easy?"

"That's not why I'm holding back."

Lane stilled. They hadn't been making much eye contact even if they were face-to-face, but Lane looked at him now. "Is this about Sam?" Parker didn't answer. Lane tapped him on his arm with a fist. "Parker!"

"You want it?"

"Obvious—"

Parker shoved it in. It was too fast, and Lane whimpered, folding into the mattress. Parker put his nose in Lane's neck. He inhaled his metallic scent, licked behind his ear. The rhythm of Lane's breathing changed. The metallic scent grew stronger.

Parker pulled back and found blood tears streaming into Lane's hair.

"Shit." Had he torn him? His knot was swelling now that it was seated; he couldn't pull it back out yet. But he reached down and felt around where they connected, felt Lane's hole stretched around him. It seemed the skin was intact; the only moisture was from Parker's cock. "We'll slow down for a minute."

"No. Feels good, I'm just—" Lane sniffed. "Will you bite me?"

Parker furrowed his brows. Maybe he should. In a few hours, he'd barely know his own name, and with a clear head, he could go easier. If one could go easy with fangs in flesh. Lane would know better than he did about that. Sam would, too.

Parker rested his elbow against the bed and stroked Lane's scalp with his claws. "Is that what you want?"

"Yes. If it means you'll fuck me like you give a shit." Lane smeared at the blood at the corners of his eyes. "If you're not going to, just come so I can go. I'm not going to stay for this if you don't care."

Guilt and indignation spurred Parker's wolf to howl beneath his skin. *Don't let him leave.* For once, Parker surrendered to the beast. "Tilt your head back."

Lane obeyed. A violent throb of arousal pulsed through Parker's cock, and his fangs ached. He gripped Lane's hair and sniffed his unmarred throat.

"Just do it," said Lane. He was panting, his hands curled around Parker's shoulders. "I want to be yours. Please."

Even though Parker was the Alpha, and Lane was the one showing his throat, Parker was powerless. He had no choice but to sink his teeth into Lane's flesh when he begged like that, and when there were no other wolves around to threaten their mating.

As soon as blood hit Parker's tongue, Lane arched, his hole clenching around Parker's knot. His skin broke out in that bloody sweat, and he moaned. "D-Don't take them out. I'll heal."

So he didn't want to heal? Parker kept his fangs embedded and thrust into him, once, twice, until Lane's voice box vibrated with a feral cry. Like a mated omega. Hot blood spurted between them.

Parker slipped his fangs out and kept thrusting, his gaze focused on Lane's slack body and hooded eyes. The holes at Lane's throat closed up, and Lane coughed.

Fill him up. Make him pregnant, fat. The wolf seemed to claw at his brain until nothing remained but the urge to breed. His was rut was upon him.

* * *

Parker seemed to disappear during the sex, which made it a lot different from how they'd made love before. Lane wasn't sure he liked it, but after a while, he disappeared too. He felt everything, but he lost time. The pleasure made him sweat. He came and came, and all the blood tried to dry, but they were both so hot. Lane's heart didn't get to rest for a long time.

At one point, fierce hunger brought Lane out of his fog. After he'd taken his fill from Parker's throat, he passed out only to wake again when Parker bit him back, his cock thrusting deep.

The sun glowed and then dimmed behind the blinds: day to dusk. Lane lay sprawled on the bed, the muscles in his open thighs aching as severe exhaustion limited his accelerated healing ability. Dusk turned to night. Maybe another two or three hours passed before Parker pulled out of Lane, mumbled something about water, and left the room.

Lane's hole throbbed. His fangs throbbed. He limbs felt weighted. Maybe before they started up again, they could bathe. And he could down a whole blood bag...

"Hey." Parker was back. He had a little blood around his lips. Lane's? He stroked Lane's cheek—covered in half-congealed blood—with clawless fingers.

"Hey," Lane croaked.

"Shower while I change the sheets?"

Lane crinkled his brow. "Is it...over?"

"No, just a break. But I didn't think you'd sweat this much."

Embarrassment made Lane feel cold. His heart was still beating, but it was growing slower, fainter. "I'm sorry."

"No, no, no. It's all right." Parker smiled and bent to kiss Lane's forehead. "I didn't think it through. Got waterproof mattress covers a couple weeks ago, though. Don't sweat it." Parker laughed at his own bad joke.

Lane managed a chuckle and propped himself up on his elbows. "Am I drinking from you or a blood bag? Starving." Not quite, but whatever would get Parker moving. And blood meant getting rid of all his aches in a matter of minutes.

"Blood bag. I'll get it for you. Uh... Do you want it warmed up?"

"Yeah, thanks."

Parker left and returned with a hot glass of blood that Lane downed immediately, moaning with pleasure as the pain started to subside. He set the empty glass on the nightstand and turned to appraise Parker's naked form. He was flaccid, and his body was covered in almost as much blood as Lane's. "You have to shower, too."

"You first. Just yell if you need anything. Heather's not here, so there's no one to disturb."

"Okay."

"Do you need help getting to the bathroom?"

Lane squinted suspiciously at Parker. "Is this because I told you to give a shit?" Lane wasn't sure Parker had been this nice *before* their fight.

"Um... Oh. No. You're my mate. Have to take care of you." Parker scratched the back of his neck.

Lane stared up at him. Hope—and satiety—locked his heart into place. To Parker, "mate" seemed to mean more than the length of the rut. He'd told him the Bond would last as long as Lane acknowledged him. But this seemed too good to be true after the abandonment.

"I can get there myself. Might take a little extra time, though. Won't use much hot water. Just want to be cold for a while, let my heart rest."

"Sure. Whatever you need."

Their gazes met awkwardly, and then Lane looked away. As he headed into the bathroom, worries swarmed in his head. Was this Bond an obligation like the one between Maker and progeny? Would it hurt Parker to be apart from him? Despite what he'd said to the contrary, would Parker be able to deny the Bond and leave like Theo had? And so on, and so on. He sat down in the tub, pulled his knees close to him, and put his head directly under the spray.

* * *

Parker should sleep. Lane was sleeping, gathering much needed rest for when Parker's rut flared up again, and Parker should have been doing the same. But he wanted a moment to revel in the fact that Lane was here, beautiful and serene, the sight of his throat no longer driving Parker to madness.

The Bond hadn't fixed things, but the warmth it had put in Parker's stomach was steadily melting the ice in his heart.

The house was quiet, peaceful. The only sounds were Parker's heartbeat and breathing as Lane slumbered like a corpse. Then, a buzzing sounded from the hallway. Parker got up to investigate and found Lane's duffel bag sitting innocuously just outside the door. Inside it, his phone was ringing. With a cautious look back at Lane, Parker reached into the bag to see who was calling.

Not Sam, thank God. Erica.

He let the call go to voicemail and then checked Lane's text messages. He had several from Erica, starting at around eight the previous night.

Where are you? We had an agreement.

I'd appreciate it if you responded.

If you don't let me know where you are before sunrise, I'll have to inform Theo.

Lane, I'm worried about you. Please answer. Are you with Parker?

Parker typed a reply. *I'm safe. Yes, I am with Parker.* Maybe Lane would think it overstepping, but Parker didn't want to get him in trouble with his Maker. The rift between them was big enough.

Thank you. Don't scare me like that again.

Parker tucked the phone back into the duffel and brought the bag into the bedroom.

"You should get a mini fridge."

Parker closed the door and looked up to see Lane blinking at him with groggy eyes. "Yeah? Why's that?"

"To put water in. And my blood bags."

"Maybe I'll get one before the next full moon."

Lane glanced at the duffel and then focused his gaze back on Parker. "Find anything interesting on my phone? My elders don't let me keep a password on it, but I didn't think I'd have to worry about *you*."

Parker fought to keep his voice even. "It's not like that. Erica was freaking out. I sent her a text." He fetched the phone and brought it with him to the bed.

Lane sat up and snatched it. After investigating, he calmed. He shut it off and tossed it across the room, where it landed on top of the duffel.

"Do you sleep at all during the rut?" he asked.

"Yes. I was just..." *watching you sleep.*

"I can sleep somewhere else."

"No."

Lane's eyes widened. Parker's own must have flashed orange. He got into bed with Lane and pulled him snug against his front. It felt both natural and unnatural being there with the one who had the power to hurt him the most—his mate.

He kissed him on the top of his blond head. "I'm sorry for dumping you. I was in pain."

"I know. But do you understand why I went to Sam?"

Nose in Lane's hair, Parker breathed in his scent. "Not really."

"I knew biting me was important to you. I couldn't stand the idea of freaking out on you when you tried. I was sure you'd break up with me."

It would have upset Parker, yes. But would he have dumped him? No. *No.* It seemed trying to make that point again wasn't worth it, though. "Okay, Lane. I understand."

"I'm sorry for hurting you. I was hoping you wouldn't find out about it at all."

Parker stroked Lane's hair. "The truth is always better than a lie, babe." He would know. He'd told Carly the truth, and it had been terrible, and sometimes he still doubted himself. But at the end of the day, he preferred this reality to the one where he pretended he loved her like she wanted him to. Anyway, he wouldn't have found Lane. "You can be honest with me."

Lane turned in his arms and searched Parker's eyes, his clear blue irises moving back and forth. "How do I know? How do I know you won't leave me like Theo did?" He put his hand on Parker's chest. "I know you say you're sorry, but you already left me once."

Oh. He hadn't quite thought about it like that. Seeing Lane's naked fear, he ached in sympathy. "Because..." Should he say it? Was it too soon? Or would it finally settle Lane, stop him from buzzing around like a panicked insect when all he had to do was be himself and let Parker fill the voids in him? He traced along the back of Lane's ear and rubbed the lobe gently. "I love you."

Lane clenched his fingers where his hand rested on Parker's chest. "Do you mean that? It's not just the Bond?"

The Bond had influence, but it couldn't make someone lie. Parker knew what lying felt like. He made his voice as smooth and steady as he possibly could. "I mean it. I love you, Lane."

Lane searched Parker's eyes for a couple more seconds before pulling him into a passionate kiss.

* * *

After three more days and a confirmation from Heather that she would remain at Rina's, Parker found a spare shower curtain in the linen closet and laid it out on the carpet in the living room. They were running out of clean sheets, and he told Lane that he didn't want any more distractions.

Lane found himself falling into the routine of the rut more easily than he or Parker had ever thought possible. Fuck, rest, rinse, and repeat. But after a few more rounds, they'd stopped even bothering with showers. During breaks, they'd sit at the kitchen table on towels, Lane sipping at a blood bag while Parker ate barely cooked steaks. The scent of stale animal blood would have made Lane lose his appetite if he hadn't needed all the human blood he could get.

Parker stopped disappearing during sex. It was a lot more like what they'd had before, only now, Parker communicated in grunts and growls, and he was rougher. He clawed Lane's hips as Lane rode him, and smacked Lane's ass hard enough to make him whine. A few times, flashes from Lane's past made appearances—sense memories from when Adrian had fucked him. They similarly took him out of the pleasure, but he always returned to it. And when he did, Parker would lick him as if he'd watched him go and now welcomed him back.

When it seemed as if Parker's rut would soon come to an end, Lane started worrying about what he had to go back to. He'd shut off his phone and hadn't bothered charging it. He didn't want to talk to Erica, Sam, or Theo. He wanted to stay with Parker, wanted to keep being ravished and loved. Maybe he could move in officially. He could bring all his shoes and clothes. He could be done with the den, with Theo, all of it. He still wasn't that good at feeding on humans, but he could survive off blood bags and Parker. It wasn't a big deal.

A sharp pain burned at Lane's side: Parker's claws. He focused on the body rocking on top of him, bringing him slowly but steadily toward climax.

"I'm here," he whispered.

Parker licked his cheek.

"I don't know if you'll remember this—" Lane continued, but Parker gripped his hand and shoved it back against the blood-smeared shower curtain, making Lane grunt. He locked his orange gaze with Lane's. Was he listening? Was he trying to shut him up? "I want to move in," said Lane. "For real."

It was impossible to tell if Parker understood him. He just kept rocking into him, blowing up the pressure in Lane's lower stomach like a balloon.

"I love you, too," said Lane. He hoped Parker wouldn't remember, because his voice cracked as he said it, and blood sprouted in his eyes. He'd told Adrian he'd loved him so many times, but Adrian had never returned the words. It had felt empty. With Parker, it was like letting go into sure arms. Parker licked the tears as soon as they fell. "I love you," Lane said again.

Later, the sun had risen again. Parker pulled out of Lane and rolled onto his back. "It's fading," he said, voice scratchy. "Think that might have been the last flare-up."

Lane rolled onto his side. "I'm kinda sad it's over."

"Not me. I'm starving." Parker grinned, and Lane laughed. "I'd love it if you moved in, by the way. I heard you."

"Yeah?" Bloody and sticky and tired as he was, Lane got on top of Parker. Elation and exhaustion were a heady mix.

"Yeah. Maybe we could get our own place."

"Theo will probably cut me off if I make it official. Me leaving the den."

"Do you want to make it official?"

Lane traced Parker's jaw. His brain wasn't up to the task of weighing all the pros and cons, so he settled for a simple "I think so."

"Then we'll figure it out."

Parker's heartbeat was strong. Lane's blood needed replenishing, and Parker hadn't fed him once this whole time... It was cruel, really. Lane tilted Parker's head back. *Nourishment*.

"Want me to be your blood bag?" asked Parker.

"Yes, please."

"Go ahead."

Even with all the pleasure Parker had wrung from his body over the past several days, desire sparked in Lane's gut as he leaned down and buried his fangs in Parker's jugular.

CHAPTER TEN

Parker's job was to talk to Heather about moving. Lane's job was to visit the den and pack up his things. Parker offered to go with him, and Lane wanted to accept the offer, but he couldn't imagine that going well. Maybe he would just go in, grab his stuff, and never come back. Maybe he wouldn't make it official like he'd said. How long could he drag out staying with Parker before he experienced repercussions? He'd done it for weeks at a time before. What about months, years?

But if he and Parker were going to really make a go of things, Lane didn't want the den at the back of his mind. He didn't want to worry that Erica and Sam—and even Theo, when he came back—would come after him and hole him up in the mansion again. They were always going to be far more powerful. They could control him if they tried.

If he was up-front about things, though—if he told them now that he was leaving the den—they might not let him leave at all.

The worry was a solid ball of lead in his chest. He fought past it as he revved up Parker's Buick and drove over to the den, but the worry nearly choked him once he got inside, carrying a couple suitcases that Parker had lent him. Classical music was playing faintly downstairs and human heartbeats thudded at different rhythms. He managed to make it to his room, but a few minutes later, a knock sounded on the doorjamb.

Erica came in and stood with her arms crossed, her high heels making imprints in the dark carpet. She wore a burgundy dress with glitter accents and dramatic wing-tip eyeliner. Lane was piling all of his socks and underwear into one of the suitcases, his fingers shaking.

"Yes?" he said irritably.

Erica sighed. "Taking the rest?"

"Of my stuff? Yeah."

"Do you want the furniture, too?"

Lane's eyes drifted furtively to the cherry dresser and bed frame. They were luxurious, but they weren't his. "No." He and Parker had talked about getting a cheap bed from IKEA, anyway. Plus, he didn't want to have to make a second trip.

Erica said, "It's yours if you want it."

"No, it belongs to the den."

"By that logic, everything you own belongs to the den. We bought it for you."

She didn't say it coldly, but it put Lane on the defensive anyway.

"Should I leave these then?" He gestured abruptly to the clothes he was packing. "I can buy new ones."

"Of course not." Erica's smooth face scrunched in concern. She uncrossed her arms and came a little closer. "How long will you be gone this time?"

There was his opening, but it was as if someone else was speaking when he answered. "That's none of your business."

"It is my business." Perhaps it was love that made her voice hard. Perhaps it was worry over losing him. Had she been giving Theo updates as Lane had assumed?

Lane looked up and pushed his shoulders back. "What if I say 'forever'?" There.

Erica's eyes lit with something cold, pained. "Have you spoken to Theo about this?"

"No. Have you? He hasn't so much as sent me a text in weeks."

"Oh, I see." Erica pressed at her hair as if she was tucking something back in place. But it was already perfect. "You want attention. Well you'll have to ask him for it yourself, I haven't told him about your little vacations."

"Why not?" Anger spurred him. He started packing in earnest, stuffing pajamas on top of his underwear and socks.

"To protect you."

Lane laughed.

Erica crossed her arms. "Do you think Theo will be forgiving for something like this? It's one thing to bed a shifter, it's another to—"

"Move in with him?"

Erica's fangs descended. Lane flinched. "I was going to say, it's another to disrespect your elders this way. If you want to go somewhere else, that is your decision, but you have gone about it in an unnecessarily hurtful way. I know we have had sparse contact, and I know you assured me you were safe, but this is—"

"You're babbling, Erica. Try to make some sense."

She recoiled as if he'd slapped her. "You have caused me pain."

Lane's chest constricted in guilty sympathy, but he clenched his jaw and kept packing.

Erica's eyes were aflame. "Theo does his best. He is a compassionate man. Sam wishes he could bed you as he has everyone else, but I am the one who truly cares for you."

"You admit it then?" Sympathy twisted into hard self-pity. "Theo doesn't care for me?"

"He does in his way. But *I* love you."

Lane knew that. She'd never said it, but he knew. And Erica had never once wanted to get under his skin or take off his clothes. Did that mean he owed her, though? He just wanted to be happy.

"If you love me, you'll let me leave the den."

"I can't do that."

Lane snapped his gaze up.

"You may stay with Parker for now. But you are too young to sever ties with the den. I will have to inform Theo. Perhaps he will allow me to come up with some sort of schedule for the rest of your training."

Lane didn't want to listen to her. But a compromise was better than anger or an ultimatum. She wasn't forcing him to stay. Maybe if he let her work it out for him, Theo wouldn't cut him off financially. It wasn't like Parker was rich. "Fine."

Erica sighed again. "Sometimes I wish I was the one who had turned you. I have never sired a progeny."

"What's stopping you?" Lane moved over to the closet.

"The pain of separation. I see you hurting, and I know Theo is hurting, even if he does not show you."

"He could tell me. We could talk; make it better. Him suffering alone doesn't help me."

"I know."

Lane transferred a pile of garment bags from the closet to the stack of packed suitcases. "Parker's good to me. Maybe one day you can meet him."

"I would like that very much. I have nothing against shifters, you know."

"Don't you?"

"No. I would worry if you were dating an older vampire as well. I would worry no matter what."

Lane got the urge to hug her, but he buried it. Somehow a hug didn't mesh with her immaculate appearance.

"I'm going to return to the party," she said. "Expect to hear from Theo in a few nights."

"All right."

She closed the door behind her, and Lane sat down on the edge of the bed, rubbing his temples with the heels of his hands. He'd crossed one hurdle, but Theo's attention was another beast. He wanted it—much less than when Theo had first left—but he was sure the conversation would be nothing but a vehicle for Theo's inevitable disappointment in him. Just like their last one, but inevitably worse.

* * *

"Really?" Parker was sitting at the kitchen table.

"Yes, really," said Heather. "This is perfect. Rina and I have been wanting to get a one-bedroom." She bit her lip and grinned at the same time. She had one foot up on the edge of her chair, her arms around a knee. "Maybe I can quit the cafe and just work at Meta."

"Yeah, maybe." Parker was inclined to think it would be perfect, too, if he and Lane kept the house after Heather moved out, as he and Heather had just discussed. But they'd have to host the shifter parties. Which meant they couldn't disappear during them. They'd have to actually...mingle. Parker could mingle, but he couldn't imagine Lane being okay with any of it. There were other options, like renting outside venues, but that got complicated quick. And if Theo did cut Lane off like Lane feared, money was going to be extremely tight. Lane was going to have to get a job. "I'll talk to Lane. I need a cigarette, though."

Heather's brows dipped in concern, but Parker ignored the look as he left. He stepped out onto the back porch and lit up.

Lane was at his den, dealing with his family. Parker hadn't talked to his since November—two months ago. He had no interest in speaking to his father or mother. They'd both shunned him when he'd told them he was more interested in men than women. But his little sister Daisy accepted him no matter what. With his free hand, he dialed her number.

It was stupid, but as soon as she answered, he started to feel sick with nerves.

"Parker? You okay?"

"Yeah. I know it's been forever, but I just wanna tell you something. Are you busy?"

"Nope." He must have paused too long. "What did you wanna talk about?"

"I..." He swallowed. "I got a boyfriend."

It wouldn't have been weird to talk about it with Heather. It shouldn't have been with Daisy, either, but...

"*What?* Did you find a male omega? Which pack is he from?"

"Uh." He laughed nervously. "No."

"Human, then?"

Parker's claws came out, and he dropped his cigarette. *Stupid.* "He's a vampire."

A pause. "Whoa."

"Yeah. D-Don't tell Mom and Dad."

She barked out a laugh. "No way, of course not."

"I actually... We're moving in together."

She laughed again, but the sound was slightly more forced. "Geez. That was fast."

"He needed a place to stay. It's good. I bonded with him."

Daisy was quiet for several seconds. "I didn't know we could do that with vampires."

"Yeah." He forced a chuckle. "Don't go looking for a vampire, though. They bite."

"Right."

"Look, I hope this doesn't stress you out. But I'm not going to be coming on any more runs. I missed the last one because of my rut, but I just can't anymore. I'm sorry."

Daisy's voice was quiet. "It's okay." Parker started to say something more, but she beat him to it. "I've decided to go to State by the way, for school. That way I can live with Mom and Dad, and they can help me through full moons and stuff." Full moons and heats. Parker tried not to think about his baby sister going out on her own, an omega in heat on a college campus. He'd had to drop out of school after two semesters. He hadn't clicked with any of the wolves he'd met there, and it was too much being a young Alpha on top of everything else. Daisy was stronger than him, though, and apparently more practical.

Parker pressed a thumb and forefinger to his temples. "You really want to live with Mom and Dad?"

"What else am I supposed to do? I'm not like Carly. I don't have a big Alpha boyfriend to protect me."

The words hit Parker like a punch, and he went quiet. He hadn't spoken to Carly, but he knew from social media she was planning to go to grad school in another state. He hadn't known she had a boyfriend. Not that he should care.

"Shit, you didn't know, did you?" asked Daisy. "But it's true. I can't go to college in another city by myself."

Parker scowled. "I could protect you. You could still go to State, but you could get an apartment, and you could come here for heats. You wouldn't have to deal with Dad's bullshit."

"I can't afford it. And Dad's fine to me, it's just you he's upset with."

She was right. But it was just a matter of time before Daisy did something to disappoint him. It was easy enough to do. Or maybe she wouldn't, because she wasn't a boy, and so far, she didn't seem interested in women.

"You could always live with me." That would be even more to put on Lane. But maybe they could—

"No. I've made my choice, and I'm fine with it. I just wanted to let you know. Okay?"

They always said younger siblings were the least responsible, but it seemed Parker was the fuckup in the family. "Okay. You want to come visit sometime though? Once Lane and I get settled?"

"Is Lane your boyfriend?" Her voice did that slightly higher-pitched delighted thing again.

Parker smiled. "Yeah."

"Of course. Maybe someday you could bring him to meet Mom."

Just Mom? Maybe. But the idea made him cringe. And Parker's dad might be an asshole, but his parents were in love. Their

Alpha/omega bond was the very definition of the thing, and maybe that was why they couldn't understand his decisions. He couldn't imagine bringing his mom into his life with Lane and not dragging in his dad, too. Dad would taint things. So he lied. "Sure."

"I love you. I gotta go, though. I have homework."

Parker smiled. His chest lifted with pride. Maybe someday Daisy would find a decent Alpha to partner with, and make everybody proud, too. Maybe she'd stand on her own two feet, either loving no one or whomever she wanted.

"All right, sis. Love you, too. Bye."

When Parker strode back into the house, he was feeling much calmer. But about twenty minutes later, Lane arrived looking like he'd seen a ghost or ten.

"Babe." Parker sat up straight from where he'd been lounging on the couch. "What's wrong?"

Lane rolled one of his suitcases into the living room and set it next to the side of the couch.

"Was it that bad?" asked Parker.

"Um." Lane crunched his brows together. "I guess not..." He sat down next to Parker, his small body compact and rigid. With his expensive black winter coat and matching gloves, he looked just like a vampire. "Theo's going to call."

"Okay."

Lane crumpled down onto his side and rested his head in Parker's lap. Parker immediately put his fingers in his hair, massaging his scalp and his pale ear.

"So you can't leave the den?" he asked softly.

"I don't know. Would you be mad if I didn't?" Lane turned his head, looking up at Parker with pleading eyes.

"Could you still live with me?"

"Yeah. At least, I think so."

Parker reached around to unbutton Lane's coat. He must be uncomfortable still wearing it. "Of course I won't be mad. I told you we'd figure it out, and we will. No matter what."

Lane relaxed again, exhaling. He gripped Parker's hand, stopping him from getting to the rest of the buttons. "Thanks. I don't know what I would have done without you these past few months."

"You would have been lost. Downtrodden. Completely bereft."

Lane laughed, but there wasn't much mirth in the sound. "You're right. Murder scene eyes for a whole year."

Parker didn't know what that meant, exactly, but he smiled. And he ripped off what part of the Band-Aid he could reach. "Heather wants to move out, and she said we could stay here. But we'd, uh...have to take over the parties."

Lane was silent for a few seconds. But then he kissed Parker's palm. "That's fine with me."

Thank God. Maybe everything really would be okay with them.

CHAPTER ELEVEN

Theo had been angry with Lane once before. Lane remembered it clearly, like a brand in his gray matter, unable to be buried with his other dark memories.

It was a couple of weeks after he'd been "born," and he'd been too new to focus on anything except blood. Theo had left him locked in his bedroom for a whole day, trying to train him to sleep when the sun was up. Erica had heard him crying, and when she'd come to check on him (against Theo's wishes), he'd bitten her. He'd been so hungry—too hungry to sleep, too hungry to care if the blood he drank was a human's or a vampire's.

Erica was fine; she was stronger and older and had managed to dislodge his teeth easily. But Lane couldn't stop, and he continued to make a real effort to get at her blood. So she'd sped to the door and only narrowly avoided smashing Lane's fingers when she slammed it shut.

Later, Theo, fresh from sleep and still in pajamas, had come to Lane. The punishment was a physical one, but very different from the experience of his death. Theo didn't once bare his fangs, but instead, commanded him to face the wall. Then he hit Lane. The whole situation was traumatic, most of all because Lane had gotten hard. After that, all of Theo's punishments had involved Lane's mind and heart.

How bad would the punishment be this time? Lane hadn't attacked any of his elders, but he'd disrespected them. He'd never so much as considered leaving the den until now, but Theo would see that as disrespect.

Lane thought when he finally got the call from Theo that he might cry and tremble. Maybe he'd feel his Maker's bond through the line and start babbling apologies. But when his phone buzzed against the coffee table, Theo's name lighting up the screen, all he felt was cold.

He picked it up. "Hello?"

Parker switched off the TV and made to stand, but Lane gripped him by the shirt hem. *Please don't leave.*

"Hello, my child."

Parker dropped back down onto the cushion, and Lane's heart started pumping in the few seconds of silence until Theo spoke again.

"Erica tells me you'd like to leave the den. Is this true?"

"Yes."

Theo's tone was even, which could mean one of two things: either he wasn't mad or that he was very mad. "I am not in the habit of bending to the whims of newborns, but your actions, in this case, warrant a talking-to. I'm afraid you've forced me to deliver an ultimatum, my child."

Lane's stomach twisted, but he remained still as stone. Parker rested a hand on his thigh.

"Lane, are you listening to me?"

"Yes, Maker."

"I can only assume this is an act of rebellion. Is this the case, or have you another reason for wanting to leave?"

Lane scoffed softly. "I have a boyfriend."

"Your shifter? Parker, right?"

"Yes. I know you don't approve, but—"

"I never said that."

"Sam did."

"Lane. I am your Maker, not Sam. Not Erica. Do you think it is easy for me to be away from you? You are causing me pain by worsening the situation."

What was it with elders, anyway? After so many years, they seemed to get comfortable saying things like: *"You are causing me pain."*

Lane fired back. "You could have taken me with you to the summit, but you didn't."

"I am trying to help you. If I coddle you—"

"No. No." Theo went quiet. Lane let the silence stretch to test it, but Theo seemed to be waiting for him to go on. He wondered, did Theo regret making him? Sometimes, in his hopeless moments, Lane regretted being born. "What's the ultimatum? Just get to the point for once."

"Fine. If you do not return to the den and remain there until I return in nine months' time, you will be cut off. You will receive no further support, financially or otherwise, from me or anyone else in the den. Not even Erica, though she weeps for you. Do you understand?"

Blood oozed from Lane's tear ducts, dripping onto his cheeks. "I understand."

"If you return home, we can discuss other options. I do not forbid you from seeing your wolf, but I do forbid you leaving your elders before you are ready. You are not ready, Lane. You need us. I will not abide this—"

"No." Lane's heart sent blood rushing behind his ears.

Theo was silent for several moments. "No?" he said eventually.

"No, I'm not coming back to the den. I don't care if you've been alive for centuries. I haven't. Nine months is a long time. Parker makes me happy, and I'm moving in with him. If you care about me at all—"

"Of course I care."

"You don't tell me you care. You don't show me." It was embarrassing, the way his voice croaked with sadness, but he knew in his chest that this was the end of things between him and his Maker. "I wish you'd never made me sometimes. You don't love me like you're supposed to. I know it." Maybe if he'd been turned by a lover, things would be different. But Theo had only saved him because it fit with his moral code, not because he had actually wanted to.

"I do love you. I do not regret making you." Theo's voice had grown colder. It was like he was sounding out the words. "One of our kind did something unforgivable, and I corrected that. But I grow weary of your childish antics. I will not have you holding an esteemed place in my den if you will not respect me as your leader and your Maker. If you have made your decision..."

He trailed off. Lane had never heard him fail to finish a sentence before.

"I've made my decision. I won't go back to the den. I'm staying with Parker." Lane's ears had started ringing, a sign that his blood pressure was rising. Part of him argued that this was a stupid decision. Parker could be gone tomorrow. And even if they did stay together, Parker was not immortal. Plus, they'd only been dating a few months and had already managed to break up and get back together. But— "Parker treats me like... He treats me like I matter. If he sees me hurting, he does something about it."

"You have not told me about your pain."

"But you know it's there!" Tears slid down to soak into the fabric of his T-shirt, but he didn't bother wiping them away. What good did it ever do? It would be just like when Parker had dumped him. He'd be a mess for days.

"Good-bye, Lane."

"You didn't call me! I called you, and I don't care how busy you are, this isn't fair. You left me alone; you ignored me. You left me to Erica, and now you're taking her away from me, too. You're heartless. You don't love me." When he paused, it was to utter silence. He pulled the phone from his ear and saw that the call had ended.

That bastard. That hardened corpse. Why had he saved Lane only to abandon him? Lane's thoughts spiraled, went dark and sick. His whole shirt would be covered in blood soon enough. He threw his phone onto the carpet.

"Hey." Parker's eyes were frantic. They darted over Lane's features as his hands came up to cup Lane's cheeks. "Lane, it's all right. It's going to be okay."

Lane swallowed. His throat felt dry. His fangs were out, but they weren't hurting. He met Parker's gaze. "I wish he'd never saved me."

"No, no, no." Parker slid onto Lane's lap, straddling him, trapping him between soft cushion and warm strength. He kissed his forehead, which only made Lane sob harder. "You'll be okay. You're not alone. Shh."

He felt alone, even with Parker here. Because Parker couldn't get it. As far as Lane new, werewolves didn't have Makers.

"It's over between me and him." Lane's arms were slack at his sides, his wrists up. "I'm out of the den. That's all that matters."

Parker kissed his cheek, his lips. Lane didn't respond. "Do you want me to leave you alone?"

"No." Was it better or worse to have Parker against him while he cried? He didn't know. So he could stay.

"I could hear most of what he said."

"Awesome."

"Do you want to go back to the den? Make him happy so you don't lose him? I'll understand."

"No." Did Parker think this was all just for him? It wasn't. "I'm not going back there. I want to stay with you."

"Okay."

Lane's cheeks itched under the coating of blood that was now drying. He gave in and wiped at them. "I'm getting blood on you."

"I don't care."

"Can I ask you a question?"

"Of course."

Lane looked past Parker at the empty, black TV screen. "Do you think we really love each other? It's not just infatuation?"

Parker's finger under Lane's chin brought his gaze back to him. "I love you. I care about you, and I want you to be happy. That's what love is."

Lane nodded.

"Do you feel that way about me?" asked Parker. "Do you want me to be happy?"

"Yes." Of course he did. That was why he'd given Parker his body, even with the possibility that his touch would bring back bad memories.

Parker held Lane's head and kissed him on the forehead again. "Do you want me to feed you?"

For the first time, Lane honestly didn't. Maybe in a few hours, he'd be hungry from all the crying, but for now, he shook his head.

"Do you want to lie down?"

Lane didn't want to move. He shook his head again.

"Do you want to stay here, like this?"

"Yes," he whispered.

Parker wrapped an arm around the back of Lane's neck and pulled him closer, whispering sweet things into his ear. "You'll be okay. You've got me. Maybe we can find you a new den if you really need one. Just 'cause somebody made you doesn't mean you have to have them in your life. I don't talk to my parents anymore, and I'm doing okay."

Lane listened, nodding along. He didn't tell Parker about how he didn't talk to his parents either, and how if he thought about *that* for more than a few seconds, he would feel it start to kill him. He used to talk to them on the phone. He still updated his Facebook so they wouldn't worry enough about him to make problems. But he couldn't see them. Not until he could control himself well enough to keep up the appearance of being alive, or come up with a good reason to keep his mother from hugging him and feeling skin that wasn't warm enough to be human. He knew they probably worried about him, but there wasn't anything he could do about that right now.

"Do you think—" His voice broke, and he cleared his throat. "Do you think you could shift for me? Be a full wolf?"

Parker stared at Lane for a moment, his brows raised. Lane wondered if it was offensive to ask him for that. But eventually Parker said, "Of course." He got up and stripped off his clothes, leaving them in a pile before fur sprouted and bones shifted, transforming him from to animal.

Lane got down onto the floor and lay on his side on the carpet. "Thanks."

Parker came over and sniffed at him before curling up next to him, the heat and softness of his furry body causing Lane's eyelids to droop.

"I always wanted Theo to fuck me."

Parker growled softly but didn't move, and his eyes and teeth were facing away from Lane.

"Actually, it was more than that, I wanted him to love me. Romantically. But he doesn't respect me even though he made me. They all think I'm a burden. Except for Erica." Fresh tears sprouted as he thought about her. "I love Erica. I'm going to miss her so much."

Parker did move then, turning around so he could lick at Lane's face. Lane tensed at the initial, too-wet feeling, but he didn't mind having the blood cleaned away. When Parker pulled back, he rested his head on his paws and just watched Lane.

"I'm so scared," said Lane.

Parker's eyes were full of feeling. He reached out a paw and tapped it on Lane's shoulder.

For some reason, the gesture hit Lane as a little ridiculous, and he laughed, even as he was crying. "I'm sorry. I don't mean to be a mess."

Parker shifted out of wolf form. He kissed Lane, nudging him onto his back. "Stop apologizing, baby."

"Okay."

It was a little weird, being fully clothed with a naked Parker on top of him, but Lane didn't exactly mind. When Parker dipped down to kiss him, he kissed back enthusiastically, moaning when Parker's tongue snaked along his fangs.

"Let me make you feel better."

Lane let his legs fall open. "Can we tie?" Parker pushed himself up on his arms and looked down at Lane with serious eyes. Lane gazed back at him. "What?"

"You've never asked for it like that before."

Lane smiled at Parker's awed expression. "You find that romantic?"

"I do." He leaned down and kissed Lane slowly, softly. "Take off your clothes." He rolled off of him, and Lane pulled off his tear-soaked shirt and shoved down his pants and boxers. Then Parker reclaimed his spot, sighing as he slid their cocks together. "Say I'm your Alpha."

Heat flared in Lane's groin. "You're my Alpha."

"Again."

"You're my Alpha." His voice cracked over the words. By the time Parker was sliding his knot into him, Lane was lost to the pleasure, but his pain at having been abandoned by Theo slithered beneath it. It would be a long time before even Parker could make him forget.

CHAPTER TWELVE

Lane checked his bank statement every day for a week, but the money stayed where it was. He used some of it to order a dresser for delivery, since Heather was taking hers, and Parker just used the closet. He also got some other things the house wasn't coming with: a couple of full-length mirrors, a wall clock, a sheet of plastic to put over the bed when he and Parker tied. He might as well use the money if it was going to disappear soon. He was too sad at this point to worry about what he might do when it was gone. He just wanted to stay in bed, with Parker.

"I might be able to get you a job at the bar. Maybe you could wait tables."

Lane laughed coolly. Parker was getting ready for work, and Lane was lying on his stomach on the comforter, browsing on his computer. He was shopping; he wasn't looking for jobs. "That's hilarious. A vampire at a shifter bar?"

"It's not like this bar is for old people. You think so many people are prejudiced, but they're not. I don't think anyone would care."

"You're an optimist. I'm a realist."

"You're a cynic, and you're depressed."

Like that was news. Lane browsed through living room decor.

"Maybe it would help you to have a job to go to. You know, as a distraction," said Parker.

"Do I look upset?" Lane was pretty sure he didn't, because he wasn't feeling much at all, at least at the moment. He added a faux-fur rug to his IKEA cart. No real fur, because that would be offensive to a shifter, right? Probably.

"I'm worried about you."

"Don't be. I'll apply to some jobs while you're gone, okay? I can pretty much work anywhere as long as I don't have to stand right next to a window or something."

"You can work after dark at the bar."

Lane gave Parker a look over the top of his laptop screen.

It must have been a particularly vicious look, because Parker raised his brows and his hands. "Fine. It's just my Alpha bullshit, I guess."

He did look hot, though. He looked hot every time he went to work, probably so he would get good tips. Right now he was wearing a black graphic tee that was just tight enough to be distracting. Lane wished they could stay in bed all night.

"Too bad you work."

Parker frowned. "I know." Lane expected him to say something like, *Well if we* both *worked at the bar...* But he didn't.

Parker came over to the bed to kiss Lane good-bye. They locked gazes, and Lane's stomach fluttered with something other than fear. *Don't go*, he wanted to say. *Call in. Stay and help me forget.*

What he actually said was, "Do you think you'll be too tired after work to...y'know? This morning wasn't enough."

Parker smiled, but his brows creased at the same time. "Am I dating a nympho?"

"No." Lane pulled away and focused on his computer, scowling. "You said I needed a distraction. That's the kind I like."

"Hey, I was just messing with you. I won't be too tired."

"'Kay."

"Lane..."

Lane pointedly did not look at him. "Have a good night." Something tight, similar to a bruising grip from an older vamp, clutched his chest. He didn't want to be alone. But Heather was working today, too, and he didn't have anyone else now.

"Bye, babe," said Parker.

Lane closed his computer and curled up on his side, listening to Parker and Heather leave the house together. He was not going to text Erica or Sam. He was not going to call Theo. He was *not*.

* * *

Parker closed the front door behind him, and he and Heather headed into the house.

"We're home!" Heather called. She went into the kitchen, but Parker froze as he registered Lane's voice through the walls. Was he talking to himself? Unlikely.

He advanced slowly to the bedroom and stopped in the doorway. Lane looked up from where he was sitting on the bed, his entire demeanor spelling "guilty," but the phone was in his lap, not against his ear.

"Who were you talking to?" asked Parker. Maybe he was irritable after dealing with drunken shifters all night. Maybe he wasn't quite in control of his wolf when it came to that piece of shit Theo. With Lane looking like he was, it had to have been him.

"No one."

"Lane." Parker shrugged off his jacket and draped it over the foot of the bed. "Thought we agreed to be honest with each other."

"I know, but—" He looked down at his phone and rubbed at the screen with his thumb. "You're going to be mad at me."

A thousand options circled through Parker's head: he'd flirted, he'd sent a sexy pic to someone, he'd— Parker put his hands over his ears and yelled, "Tell me! You're making whatever it is worse."

"I-I gave him the address."

Parker lowered his hands and frowned at Lane. "What? Spit it out. Seriously."

"I gave Theo our address. He wants to come here."

Theo. In their house? An ancient vampire was going to waltz into a house owned by shifters. Thus far Theo had been a figment, an idea. He wanted to be real now?

"No fucking way," said Parker.

"But I already said he could."

"Without asking me *or* Heather!" Lane flinched at Parker's volume, but Parker couldn't find it in him to care right now. Jesus Christ. *Theo* was coming? Something like fear slithered down his spine. Would he ruin this for them? Would he take Lane away?

"He just wants to meet you."

Parker headed into the bathroom; he needed a shower. Lane followed at superspeed.

"That sounds like bullshit," said Parker. He stripped off his shirt and went to unbuckle his belt, but Lane stopped him with lukewarm hands on his wrists.

"Wait—"

Parker pushed Lane backward, pinning him to the sink counter.

"I knew you'd be mad," said Lane, breathless. "But I couldn't— He asked, and I just— I told him. It's the Bond."

Parker settled a hand on the back of Lane's neck and gripped. Not too hard, but enough that he'd feel it. "What if he asks you to do something else I don't like?"

In Lane's gaze, confusion morphed to insolence. "He wouldn't."

"Are you sure? You move in with me, he comes all the way back from wherever he is..."

"Switzerland."

"He comes from *Switzerland* to, what?" Parker pressed his naked thigh between Lane's pajama-clad legs. "Take you back to the den?"

Lane leaned into Parker a little, the tip of his nose brushing Parker's cheek. "He just wants to meet you. Like I said."

"Maybe he should learn how to make a Skype call."

"He's old-fashioned."

Parker lifted one of Lane's legs and ground into him, earning a few soft pants of breath against his face. "Does he want you?" Parker whispered.

"No."

"How do you know?" Lane turned his head, squirmed, but Parker slid his hand to Lane's chin and forced his gaze up. "How do you know?"

"It's an embarrassing story." Parker stilled, just stared, until the words finally came. "He punished me, I got hard, and he didn't like it. That's all."

Parker grinned, his fangs extending. He watched Lane's gaze for signs of panic and fear. "'Punished' you?"

"With a belt." Lane's heart thudded through the room, pinking his cheeks.

Parker took a step back. "Undo mine."

"Huh?"

"Undo my belt for me."

Lane only hesitated for a second before doing as Parker asked, his fingers shaky on the brown leather. Once he'd undone the buckle, he looked up at Parker uncertainly.

"Slide it out of my belt loops."

Again, Lane obeyed.

"Now, fold it in half and hand it back to me."

Lane's cheeks and ears were dark red as he put the belt in Parker's clawed fingers.

"You gonna sweat from this?" Parker taunted.

"I don't know," said Lane.

"Turn around." It was like things moved in slow motion. They were isolated, even if Heather was somewhere in the house, able to hear them. The bathroom was door was open, but Parker's senses stopped where Lane's body ended. He tightened his grip on the belt in his hands. "Did Theo make you pull your pants down?"

Lane was leaning with his hands on the edge of the counter. "No. Vampire strength makes—"

Parker brought the belt down hard against Lane's right buttock. It made a dull, thuddy sound, and Lane exhaled harshly. "Did he do it like that?"

"Yeah."

"How many times did he hit you before you got hard?"

"Three, I think."

Parker hit him twice more, delighting in the way Lane's lean muscles tensed and relaxed beneath his flushed skin. He moved in closer against Lane's back and felt him up through his pajama pants. "Yeah," he said against Lane's ear. "You're hard all right." And he was so warm. "Push down your pants for me."

Lane shoved his pants down so that they pooled around his ankles. Parker dragged the leather over his bare ass.

"Did he touch you like this?" Parker was pretty certain he knew the answer, but he wanted to hear it from Lane's lips.

"No," Lane whispered.

Parker stepped back once again to give Lane more hits. He was gentler now that there was no fabric protecting Lane's skin, but he built up the intensity as he went, as Lane's ass get redder and redder. He stopped when blood bloomed from Lane's pores.

He hadn't been able to make him do that without knotting him first.

He unbuttoned his jeans and kicked them and his boxers off, moving up against Lane's back and settling his curved-up cock between Lane's ass cheeks. He licked a stripe up Lane's spine between his shoulder blades. "You want my cock?" Lane seemed only able to nod. "You want my knot stretching you? You want my bite making your throat burn and—"

"Yes! Just claim me. I know that's what this is."

Parker shoved his cock into Lane, up to where the swell of his knot started, and Lane keened. "That's right," said Parker. "As soon as Theo sees you, he's going to know just how well-fucked you are."

Lane fell silent again aside from his moans and heavy breathing. Parker thrust until sliding in and out got easier. Then he edged his knot in, and Lane gasped as his hole stretched around it.

"I'm gonna come," he said.

Parker wrapped his claws around Lane's throat and kissed his neck as he fucked him. He met Lane's helpless gaze via the medicine cabinet mirror. Lane didn't have to beg for the bite because his eyes said everything.

Parker sank his teeth into him, and Lane's whole body tensed as he came. Then he was all relaxed warmth, a willing body for Parker to keep thrusting into.

Theo would never have this with Lane. As Parker bent him over the sink, his claws making dents in the bloody skin of his back, he had never been so sure of anything. No one would have this kind of intimacy with Lane—no one but *him*.

* * *

Lane was lying in bed—Parker had fallen asleep next to him, and Heather was finally gone from the house for good—but he was wide-awake, thinking about Theo. Was Lane a bad boyfriend, wanting to text Theo to ask him exactly when he was coming? He'd said "in a few nights," but a week and a half had passed with no visit.

In the meantime, Heather and Rina had found a new place, and Heather had been transporting boxes gradually until a bunch of big burly shifters showed up one day to help her load the rest into a truck. Parker helped, but since they'd done it during the day when the sun was high, Lane had stayed indoors. Afterward, when they were all having a few shots, he'd sat on Parker's lap on the couch, which Heather claimed she didn't need in her new apartment.

Now, lying with Parker's arms around him, casual but possessive, Lane couldn't forget about Theo's impending visit. Why did he almost always have to be the one to reach out to Theo? Why could he never find satisfaction in a cold shoulder like he could with Erica? He should be furious with how Theo had treated him, how he had given him that ultimatum and then, with a second follow-up call, turned around and demanded to see him and meet Parker, in their home.

Lane hadn't had to contact Theo that time. He'd been thinking about it, and then his phone had buzzed. It was as if his desperate thoughts had finally made manifest his secret wishes.

Theo had been sweeter than ever before. *"I apologize, my child. I sincerely regret my extreme reaction to what was clearly a cry for help. You need me. I understand that now."* Lane would have given him anything he wanted after words like that.

And he had. He'd let him in. Now, all he wanted to do was talk more.

Even though he was risking waking Parker, Lane grabbed his phone off the nightstand and sent Theo a text. *When are you coming?* It was daytime in Switzerland, if Theo was still in Switzerland. Maybe he'd already come home and was at the den, and Lane was losing out on seeing him. It would make sense for him to visit Erica first. She was essentially his second-in-command. But—

Soon, my child.

Lane clamped his eyes shut and willed his tightening chest to relax. Parker might waken if he heard his heartbeat, might think something bad was happening. But everything was fine. Everything...was...fine.

He let himself look at the text again. "Soon." Really? What was his issue with giving a day and time? Lane would have settled for a ballpark seven-day stretch at this point.

I need to know when. When do you land in Detroit?

As yet, I am unsure. The summit organizers are being slow to grant my request for leave.

What if they don't grant it?

They will. You must be patient.

Lane put his phone back on the nightstand. Theo wasn't coming. More promises, more of Lane not having a single say or hope for attention.

Next to him, Parker moved. "Everything okay?"

Lane turned to face him. At least he hadn't started by asking Lane who he'd been texting. He could have been browsing the internet or talking to Heather, even if it was well past three a.m. "Just having trouble falling asleep."

"Here." Parker, eyes closed, pressed his wrist to Lane's lips. When Lane didn't immediately bite him, Parker said, "'S'okay, babe. Go ahead."

Lane relaxed and wrapped his arm around Parker's strong forearm like it was a teddy bear. Then he did bite down. Once again, Parker reminded him in a painful moment that he was the one who offered sustenance, honored promises, and cared.

CHAPTER THIRTEEN

"You really need *eight* steaks?" Lane's voice floated from the kitchen to the bathroom, where Parker was shaving over the sink. "Can we afford that?"

"Have to," said Parker. "Full moon's coming up." He paused with the razor in midair, listening for further protests regarding the grocery list he'd given Lane. But then came the sound of the door opening and closing. He resumed shaving.

About five minutes later, the door sounded again. Parker rinsed the razor and towel-dried his face before heading out into the hallway. "Forget something?" No answer.

He crossed into the living room, moving past the kitchen—

"Hello, werewolf."

The polite words were such a shock to Parker's system that both his fangs and claws extended at the same time. He rounded on the figure standing near the kitchen table in a long black coat and gloves very similar to Lane's. He had a head of slick, dark curls, high cheekbones, and umber eyes.

"No need to take up arms," said the man, who held up two elegant hands. "I'm no threat to you."

He was gorgeous—terrifyingly beautiful.

Theo.

"What do you want?" Had he timed his visit to coincide with Lane's leaving? It seemed too convenient to be incidental.

Theo smiled, showing straight white teeth. "Do you have time to talk?"

Parker glanced at the clock on the stove. "I have to leave for work in twenty minutes."

"That will do." Theo gestured to one of the seats at the kitchen table. "May I sit?"

"Fine." They sat down at opposite ends.

Silence descended, and Theo's pleasant expression faltered. "Lane tells me you treat him very well."

"I treat him better than you do." It occurred to Parker he should be polite—if he wasn't, that could cause problems for him and Lane—but it was asking too much. When Lane had told him Theo would be visiting, he hadn't imagined he'd be talking to him alone.

"With all due respect, you aren't contending with the same circumstances."

"You mean the Bond?"

"Mm."

"I've bonded with him, too."

Theo's brows furrowed. "To my understanding, your Bond is one-sided."

"Did Lane tell you that?" Parker tried to keep his cool in this moment, but only to save face. The one-sidedness of his Bond with Lane had nothing to do with its strength or validity. Screw Theo.

"Parker." Theo steepled his fingers. "I am simply—"

"If your two-sided Bond is what caused Lane to turn into a crying mess, then I prefer the one I have with him. I take care of him. You—"

"I am not contesting you!"

Parker huffed.

In a calmer voice, Theo said, "He is all yours, shifter."

"Good," Parker growled.

"I am simply here to check up on him, and to iron out some den business. When he comes back, I will do that, but I want to—"

"'When he comes back?'"

Theo waved a hand in the air. "From wherever it was he was driving to."

Of course. Parker glanced at the clock again. Ten minutes. Would he lose his job if he called in? Could he bear to leave Lane alone with Theo? He wasn't sure if it was jealousy that made him uncertain, or the memory of Lane bawling his eyes out after Theo had given him that ultimatum.

"I want to assure you that provided you continue to treat him as well as he says, your relationship will have my blessing. I will not interfere."

Parker leaned back in his chair. An eerie calm came over him. "As if you haven't already?"

"Excuse me?"

"You and his other elders are a constant issue with us. He wants to leave the den, but he's scared about the money. Are you going to cut him off?"

Theo picked a piece of phantom lint off his pristine coat. "No."

"Are you going to let him stay here?"

"I am. But he'll have to come to the den for his training. He is not yet able to feed on a human with the proper amount of control."

"I feed him."

Theo's gaze snapped up. *"He* is immortal. You are not. These are basic skills he must master, and Erica is equipped to teach him."

"Why aren't *you* teaching him?" Parker knew why—the summit. But the opportunity to needle him was irresistible.

Theo spoke with dignified force. "I shall be returning whence I came. Lane will have everything he needs. An affectionate and knowledgeable mentor, funds, and you." Theo stood abruptly, his chair legs scraping against the linoleum.

Parker mirrored him. Pride spread through the breadth of his shoulders and settled in his groin. He grew semi-erect, but Theo was staring at his face. Parker wouldn't have minded if Theo had noticed he was getting hard; this was just another way in which he was better.

"Don't you have work to be getting to?" asked Theo.

Parker glanced at the clock again. "Yes."

"I shall wait outside for Lane's return."

Parker grabbed his keys and followed Theo out the door. He assumed Lane had failed to lock it earlier, maybe because he was used to powerful people being around. Parker, on the other hand, secured it. He was about to leave when a thought niggled: he might not get the chance to speak to Theo alone again. Should he tell him what Lane couldn't seem to say himself?

"You didn't mention yourself in the list of things Lane will have." It was like forcing himself to swallow rotten game.

Theo stood on the porch with his hands clasped in front of him. "I am always here for him."

"I don't think he feels that."

Theo smiled. "In time, he will understand. Affection gets harder, not easier. Perhaps that is why we keep shifters out of our dens. You seem to have no trouble with this...outward loving."

Parker frowned. Was that what it was really like? Theo wanted to love Lane, but couldn't? Parker tried not to think about what else he might want. Theo had said he wasn't trying to contest Parker's claim.

"You're right. I don't have trouble with that."

Parker left Theo standing there on the porch, a melancholy statue. Part of him ached in empathy for Lane, who would never get what he really needed from Theo. But another part of him tried not to take too much pleasure in the fact that even if some small part of Lane still wanted Theo romantically, he would have to take Parker instead.

* * *

Lane needed to buy a car. Yes, he'd asked Parker to give him something to do—being bored in the house all the time was going to kill him—but as he stood in the checkout line, he wasn't sure he'd be able to fit everything into his duffel bag: eight steaks, four fifths of vodka, a sack of potatoes, a gallon of milk. If he couldn't fit it all, probably he could buy another bag...

But he managed. He even walked at a human pace for a while, the duffel slung over his shoulder, listening to the sounds of traffic and the constant thrum of heartbeats, some close, some far away. The night air was frigid, so most of the humans were hidden away in their cars and houses. It was peaceful. In fact, the closer he got to the house, the more at peace he felt, until he was sleepy. Never had he felt the urge to nap before ten p.m., not since he'd been turned.

By the time he reached the mouth of the alley, he was ready to collapse right there on the gravel.

"Lane."

The voice was soft, controlled. Lane lifted his heavy eyelids to the speaker.

Maker, his instincts whispered.

Theo strode forward, down the steps off the back porch, and Lane took off the duffel bag and dropped it to the ground.

"Maker." His voice was distant, choked. Emotion erupted in his chest. He fell onto his knees and looked up at Theo in his black coat.

"My child." Theo cradled Lane's cheeks with featherlight, trembling hands. He was smiling from ear to ear. But Lane was crying, and his heart beat to push the blood out, clouding his vision. "We must go inside," said Theo.

"No." Lane grabbed at Theo's hands, trying to keep him close. "Don't stop touching me. Please, please." His very being begged for the attention. He had been starving, and now there was food just within reach.

"I'm not leaving."

"Please!" Lane yanked on Theo's arms. He needed to be lying down with him, forehead to forehead, hands in hands. The yearning made him ache, but he couldn't articulate it, couldn't tell Theo what he needed.

"It's all right." Theo got down on his knees, too. Lane scrambled to hold his face, bringing their skulls together. "Shh," said Theo. Carefully, he lowered them both onto their sides, face-to-face. Foreheads touching.

"Yes," Lane hissed. He squeezed Theo's hands.

"I know. Try to relax."

But Lane's heart was trying to flee his body and burrow itself into Theo's. He wanted to become one with him. Theo's heart was so still.

"You don't feel this."

"Shh."

It was like every other time the Bond had sunk its teeth in. Lane missed Theo even though he was right here. His body screamed; the skin over his cranium ached because he was pressing it so hard into Theo's. He couldn't squeeze his fingers tightly enough. If he'd been older than Theo, the bones would have snapped.

"It hurts. I hate this."

"What—" Theo cleared his throat. "What do you want?"

Another desire Lane could not articulate. But then, Theo had never asked him that point-blank before. What did Lane want? Six months ago, he would have said, *"Sex. Penetrate me."* He would have wanted to be as close to him as possible. Now? Sex was for Parker. And if Parker were right here, Lane wouldn't be missing him. He'd just...be.

"I want you to make the Bond go away," he said.

"That isn't possible. But it will fade with time."

"That's not good enough! You have to make it better."

"I can't. I thought..." Theo was almost always perfectly articulate. "I thought if I went away... But clearly, I was wrong."

Lane's Bond-addled consciousness had a hard time comprehending. "You..." He clamped his eyes shut and dug his nails into Theo's hands. "You left *because* of me?"

"Yes, but—"

Lane let loose a guttural cry. Then suddenly he was on his back, Theo's hand over his mouth. The shock silenced him.

"You mustn't call attention to us," said Theo. Lane shoved at him. "Stop." Theo pinned one of his hands. "I am trying my best, Lane."

Lane wanted to tell him his best wasn't good enough, but his hand was still over his mouth.

After a few moments of silent staring, Theo finally let up. Lane got to his feet, grabbed the duffel, and ascended the back-porch steps to unlock the door. Once inside, he turned to close it, but Theo was there, stopping it with his hand.

"Do you want me to stay?" he asked. "I'll not return to the summit if that is preferable to you."

Lane laughed and grew nauseous at the same time. "You're unbelievable." Had he not been wishing for that since Theo had left? "You're doing this because I want to leave the den."

"Yes."

"Is that the only reason?"

Theo scoffed softly and turned his head. "No."

"Then why?"

After a few beats, Theo returned his focus to Lane, his eyelashes fluttering. Otherwise, he was back to being as composed as ever. "It's uncomfortable being away from you. I spoke to Parker—"

"What?"

"Just listen to me. Please." When Lane didn't interrupt again, he continued, "Parker says you don't feel my affection. I struggle with this. It is a deficiency of many older vampires, but I admit that I didn't excel at it in life. I…" He dipped his brows, a delicate *V* marring his forehead. "I require your feedback in order to—"

"Hug me." Lane set the duffel down again.

"Lane. I'm not sure that's—"

"You want my feedback? Hug me."

Theo stepped into the house. He looked as if he were about to put his head on the executioner's block. But Lane waited patiently for him, curious what he would do.

Eventually, Theo came close and wrapped his arms around him.

Lane hugged him back. "Now tell me what you're thinking."

"I was thinking how small you are."

That brought a twitch to Lane's lips. He closed his eyes and tried to relax in Theo's arms, and he started to feel like he had when walking home. Peaceful, tired.

"Will you lie down with me?" he asked.

"Yes," said Theo.

Lane made sure the door was closed before leading Theo into the bedroom. He kicked off his shoes and went toward the bed. "You can put your coat wherever."

Theo unbuttoned it and shrugged it off his well-formed shoulders. Lane's stomach did flutter, but he couldn't help it. It would only be cuddling. If Parker got mad, well... They'd just have to work through it.

Theo took off his shoes before reclining next to Lane, settling on his back.

Lane cuddled up to his side and rested his cheek on his shoulder. "I don't want you to go back to the summit, but I'm going to keep staying here with Parker."

Theo swallowed. "Understood. I shall stay in the area. You will visit the den regularly, however, so that Erica and Sam and I can keep a close eye on your development."

"Okay."

"We...*I*...love you."

The words hung in the room like mist. It would only take a dry gust of wind to blow them back into the ether, but Lane grabbed onto them as best he could. "I love you, too," he whispered.

Theo touched Lane's cheek in that same faltering way, as if he were touching parchment that might tear at the slightest pull. Lane closed his eyes. At some point, his body had stopped screaming, and now his heart was locking itself into place.

Half-asleep, Lane mumbled, "I'm glad you came back."

"As am I, my child. As am I."

* * *

Parker didn't know what he'd find when he got home. Lane in tears, heartbroken? Would it be worse than before, when he'd talked about never having been turned? He couldn't imagine it going well with Theo, despite the vampire's good intentions.

He was so tight with nerves as he parked the Buick in the driveway that he thought he might shift out of stress. But everything outside the house, at least, spelled calm. He found the back door unlocked, but that wasn't unusual for Lane. In the living room, he found Lane's duffel bag.

It was filled with meat and milk that had been out for far too long. Parker sniffed it all and found it to be as yet unspoiled. He took it into the kitchen.

Everything was dead quiet and dark.

Lane must be in the bedroom. Maybe Theo had already left. When Parker got to the open doorway, however, he saw Lane was not alone. He and Theo, both fully clothed, were lying on top of the covers. Lane appeared to be sleeping, but Theo fixed his dark gaze on Parker. Then he nodded.

"I'm no threat to you," he had said. Perhaps it was the truth. Lane certainly did look peaceful wrapped around him, and Parker knew that romantic love couldn't solve every problem. He'd tried to do that for Lane, but Theo was important. Erica and Sam were important. Just as Daisy was important to him, and Heather to the both of them.

Letting out a breath, he nodded back.

It looked like he was going to be sleeping on the couch tonight.

EPILOGUE

Lane's instincts had been whispering, *threat, threat,* since the party had started. He ignored them just as he'd ignored his other stupid fears: *Every shifter except for Parker and Heather hate you,* for instance. And, *This party is going to be a disaster.*

It wasn't going to be a disaster. It was going to be just fine.

In fact, vampires and shifters were already interacting and nobody had bled yet. Erica was sitting on the couch with Rina, talking animatedly with her well-manicured hands like she did sometimes when she was nervous. And Rina, who had looked like a ghost when she'd arrived, was actually cracking a hesitant smile. There were a couple of vampires Lane knew only by face, ones Erica had brought along and who'd usually attended to their den parties. Lane spotted them easily from his place in the kitchen doorway, following the sounds of their nervous hearts. Bless them, they were staying even though the shifters scared them, and they were mingling, too.

Theo wasn't in attendance, as he'd gone back to Switzerland for the remainder of the summit. But he'd promised that when he returned, if the parties were still going (without any violent incidents), he'd try and make an appearance.

"Hey, you," said Heather, coming up behind Lane and ruffling his hair. "Where's your Alpha?"

Lane ducked away from her and smoothed back his bangs. "The store. Apparently, I didn't get enough alcohol."

"You didn't." Heather held up a fifth of whipped cream vodka, or at least, one inch of a fifth.

"He'll be back soon." In fact, Lane could hear car wheels crunching gravel outside.

"Good. I want to make White Russians. Can vampires have milk?"

"Uh... Better offer them an alternative."

Heather grinned and downed the rest of the fifth. "You got it." Then she dropped the bottle into the recycling bin and started lining up empty glasses on a tray.

Parker came into the kitchen a few minutes later, carrying plastic bags full of liquor. "Are you hiding in here? You promised you wouldn't hide, babe."

"I'm not hiding," said Lane. "Heather's in here." She rolled her eyes. "I'm *watching,* making sure everything stays under control."

"You need to relax. Do some shots with me."

"No, I don't think so."

"Why not?" Parker opened up a bottle of peach vodka and poured two shots despite Lane's protests.

"I don't want to be drunk. It's not right for the hosts to be drunk."

"We're not going to be *drunk,* we're going to be chill. And you need to chill." From where he stood at the counter, Parker gave him a look over his shoulder. "I can feel your heart pumping from here."

So what if his heart was alive? If anything, he fit in better this way. "I'm just stressed," he said, his voice a whine.

"I know, baby." Parker had taken to speaking to Lane like this when he was upset: at once smooth, comforting, and condescending. It was the same voice he used after he hit him with his belt, and it made Lane's skin break out in goose pimples that weren't anything like the ones from fight-or-flight. "C'mere," he said. "I'll take your shot for you, but I want you close." Parker had also taken to demanding intimate physical contact between them whenever possible.

Drawing close as commanded, Lane slipped his fingers into Parker's. With his free hand, Parker downed the two shots of vodka. Then he kissed Lane, tasting like peaches on fire.

"We should...go be good hosts." He sounded weak to his own ears. "We have to make sure people are having a good time."

Heather scoffed good-naturedly. "I think they'll be fine for a few minutes."

Parker kissed down Lane's throat. "She's right. Our guests can take care of themselves." He kissed Lane's ear. "But we can join the others, if it'll make you feel better."

They went into the living room, hand in hand. Parker started up a game of cards with Erica, Rina, and a shifter Lane didn't know. Lane leaned into his side the whole time and listened to their chatter, smiling whenever somebody got excited. He watched shifters and vampires make awkward but willing introductions and laughed to himself when a vampire made a face after trying one of Heather's White Russians.

In the end, when the guests were leaving, many of them thanked Lane and Parker, with some of them expressing hopes for more parties in future.

As soon as they locked the door after the last guest, Parker pulled Lane toward the hallway.

"Hey!" said Lane playfully, slapping Parker away. "We need to clean up."

"But I want to try something. I've been thinking about it all night."

"Okay." He followed Parker into the bedroom. "So what is it?"

"I need to be inside you first."

The frank language had Lane blushing; his heart had been going all night. He stripped off his clothes along with Parker and ended up where Parker directed him: on the bed beneath him, his legs bent up, and Parker against his stomach and chest.

"Tell me," said Lane, giggling.

Parker nudged his hole with the head of his cock. "Are you hungry?"

"Mmm... I could eat."

Parker kissed him, their fangs bumping into each other. "I want you to bite me at the same time I bite you."

"On your throat?"

"Mhm."

Lane's fangs ached at the idea. "Yes."

Parker slid his cock into him. Lane wasn't loose enough for the knot yet, but he would be soon enough. "Are you ready?" asked Parker.

"Ready," said Lane.

"As soon as you feel my teeth."

"Yes," Lane whispered.

They kissed. Parker peppered kisses across Lane's jaw and down his neck. No teeth yet. Lane shivered in anticipation. Another aching throb hit his fangs.

"I said I was—"

Fangs. Lane unhinged his jaw and clamped down into Parker's flesh. Hot, savory blood oozed onto his tongue at the same time that pain bloomed across his throat. He nearly came from the sensation. Parker kept his teeth embedded and thrust at a steady rhythm, creating gentle friction against Lane's cock, which was sandwiched between his own smooth stomach and Parker's. At the same time, the girth inside him inched closer to where he needed it to hit. If only Parker's knot would just go in. *Please, please, please, please...* He felt it start to stretch him. His legs shook. The blood was making him sleepy, but the pleasure racked him, its epitome just out of reach. Parker's furred chest brushed against his sensitive nipples.

Fearing he'd lose consciousness before he came, Lane pulled his fangs out of Parker's flesh. Parker mirrored him. They looked into each other's eyes, both of their mouths covered in blood.

"I love you," said Parker.

"I love you," said Lane.

Parker pressed his right hand—the *V* between thumb and index finger—to Lane's throat and thrust his hips hard, shoving his knot into him. Lane's hole stretched to accommodate the intrusion and then clamped down on it, locking them together. Parker's cock nudged his prostate. It only took two more thrusts for Lane to fall apart, sweat slicking all over his body and an involuntary cry breaking from his throat as he came.

For a moment, he was nothing but a vessel for the most intense pleasure of his life. Then the exhaustion fell over him like a heavy blanket.

Parker was still thrusting, still holding Lane under the jaw with a bruising grip. His mouth was open, and his fangs glistened with spit and blood.

Lane watched him. He kept his eyes open for as long as he could. As soon as Parker shot inside him, he let them close and drifted off, unafraid.

ABOUT THE AUTHOR

Lyssa Dering is an author of queer erotic romance. She writes about damaged characters in impossible situations who, despite often horrifying struggles, will always get their happy ending.

Email: lyssadering@gmail.com
Website: http://lyssadering.com
Facebook:
http://facebook.com/profile.php?id=100013162894226
Twitter: http://twitter.com/lyssadering
Pinterest: http://pinterest.com/lyssadering
Goodreads: http://goodreads.com/lyssadering
Wattpad: http://wattpad.com/user/lyssadering

NINESTAR PRESS, LLC

www.ninestarpress.com

www.ingramcontent.com/pod-product-compliance
Lightning Source LLC
Chambersburg PA
CBHW020342260626
47156CB00004B/1658